'EXPECTATION
(PRATEEKSHA)

'EXPECTATION' (PRATEEKSHA)

By

Rajkumari Sharma
(Hindi Edition)

&

Translated by

Dr. V. K. Goswami
(English Edition)

Published Internationally by

Powered by G Gullybaba

PENDOWN PRESS

Powered by Gullybaba Publishing House Pvt. Ltd.,
An ISO 9001 & ISO 14001 Certified Co.,
Regd. Office: 2525/193, 1st Floor, Onkar Nagar-A, Tri Nagar,
Delhi-110035
Branch Office: 1A/2A, 20, Hari Sadan, Ansari Road,
Daryaganj, New Delhi-110002
Ph.: 09350849407, 011-27387998
E-mail: info@pendownpress.com
Website: PendownPress.com

First Edition : 2012

Reprint Edition: 2016

ISBN: 978-93-81066-16-4

Dedicated
to the clan of the women who accepted the odds
as a challenge and struggled through.
&
In the holy memories of
my
Mother ('Maa') and my husband Sri. Dwarka
Nath Goswami

Preface

The novel 'EXPECTATON' ('PRATEEKSHA') written by Smt. Rajkumari Sharma is worth to be included in the list of the best novels ever written on the INDO-PAK partition.

The author in her autobiographical novel has beautifully depicted the customs, traditions, festivals, the life- style and the changing scenario in the work culture of the then Punjab. Since the author herself being a victim of the INDO-PAK partition' has undergone the horror, hence, she has succeeded in depicting the heart-breaking experience of the bloody-partition. The heroine of the novel Sita never surrenders to the adversities, never compromises to wrong ethical values but, takes them up as the challenge faces them boldly and becomes victorious. As a social-novel, it's story is very inspiring, interesting and indulging. I am confident that this novel written in simple language would be a guide & enrich the knowledge of the readers.

-Dr. Tilak Raj Goswami

About the Author
(Hindi Edition)

Rajkumari Sharma

Date of Birth: September 7, 1930; Jamki Chima' Distt. Sialkot (Now in Pakistan)

Education: M.A (Hindi) ; M.A (Pol. Science); B. Ed.

Field of work aughte

After the INDO-PAK partition, she worked first as a school teacher in the legendary land of AALAH – UDHAL, VIRBHUMI MAHOBA and later in the Department of Education, Madhya Pradesh. For the first ten years, she served as a teacher and later for 23 years, she had been the Principal of School. She inherited inspiration of writing from her God-daughter ('Dharamputri'), Urmila, the famous Punjabi poet 'Prem Lahri' (love Waves) her maternal-uncle Pt. Tulsi Ram Sharma and her younger renowned literary ('Varistha Sahityakar') Dr.Tilak Raj Goswami. At home, she persistently got the whole-hearted support from her son Wing Commander Virendra Kumar Goswami and daughter-in-law Shashi Goswami.

Address: AKANKSHA; 91-C/8, Sarvodyanagar, Bhardwaj Puram, Allahabad-211006 (U.P) Ph: 605292

F-82, Sector-41,NOIDA-201303, INDIA (Present)

About the Translator
(English Edition)

Prof. (Dr.) V.K. GOSWAMI, Ph.D. (IIT), M.S. (USA), M.Sc, PDF(USA), LL.B

Visiting Scientist: UNIDO, ICTP, ITALY

Expert Panel, NOAA, UNV, I CAO & AIU Rosters Vice Chancellor

The Hindi classic 'Prateeksha', written by the eminent writer Mrs. Rajkumari Sharma, presents the pathetic condition of the people who bore numerous sufferings because of the bloody political division of the country. It is a powerful work of fiction, which has been translated into English in a very lucid language by the eminent scholar and a scientist of great repute, Prof. (Dr.) Virendra Kumar Goswami.

Dr. V.K. Goswami, did his Ph.D. from Indian Institute of Technology, Kharagpur MS from the University of Wisconsin, USA, Post Doctorate Fellowship at the University of Illinois, Chicago, USA. He is a 'Visiting Scientist' to United Nations Industrial Development Organization (UNIDO), ICTP, Italy, Expert panelist International Civil Aviation Organization, Canada, and United Nations.

Dr. Goswami worked at Space Science Engineering Centre, NOAA (National Oceanic Atmospheric Administration) at University of Wisconsin, USA. Presented

Papers in the field of Chemical Technologies, Atmospheric Sciences, Space Sciences, Satellite Communication and Information Technology at International and National conferences held in India, USA, Latin America, South Africa, Canada and Europe. He is having 40 years of teaching, research and administrative experience at Home and Abroad.

Dr. V.K. Goswami has been an Expert panelist of Association of Indian Universities, a national level accreditation body, Wing Commander in the IAF; Director General of Management Institutes, Founder Director/ Director of many Engineering. Institutes for more than a decade before taking over the present assignment of Vice Chancellor. He was special Invitee by the World Meteorological Organization of United Nations, Geneva in 2001. He headed various delegations at National and International levels including International Conference on Metering held at Sao-Paulo BRAZIL, in 2003, and in Jun 2005 the FEMA-Higher Education Conference on Emergency/Disaster Management at Emmetsburg, USA and Chaired session SSC-2006 in, Czech Republic & Presented Research Paper on Control of Global Warming at ESF Conference, 6-11 Jun. Innsbruck, Austria 2009 and France 2010 .

He was special Invitee by the World Meteorological Organization of United Nations, Geneva in 2001. He headed various delegations at National and International levels & worked at SSEC, NOAA, USA.

Acknowledgement

It is my first and fore most duty to acknowledge my profound thanks and heartful gratitude to Mrs. Raj Kumari Sharma, the author of 'Prateeksha' (Expectation), for giving me her kind consent to translate this wonderful literary work of Hindi into English.

I am profoundly grateful to all those people without whose constant encouragement and invaluable guidance, it would not have been possible for me to have successfully translated this wonderful creation of literature.

I am greatly indebted to my wife, Mrs. Shashi Goswami and my children for their continued and sustained support and the pains they have taken in the completion of this work.

I wish to express my gratitude to Prof. Vinay Kumar Sharma, Department of English. BITS Bhiwani for his whole – hearted involvement in editing this magnificent creation.

Finally, I extend my thanks and gratitude to Mr. Ashok Kumar Rohilla for his painstaking efforts in turning this manuscript into print.

-Dr. V. K. Goswami

Contents

Preface	*vii*
Acknowledgement	*xiii*
Part-1	1
Part-2	7
Part-3	9
Part-4	13
Part-5	15
Part-6	19
Part-7	23
Part-8	27
Part-9	31
Part-10	33
Part-11	39
Part-12	45
Part-13	49
Part-14	59
Part-15	67
Part-16	71
Part-17	75
Part-18	81
Part-19	87
Part-20	89
Part-21	93

1

As the month of August commences, the heart and soul of Sita starts palpating like electric waves and the achievements, adversaries of her life starts emerging in the mind. This month is like the two bonds of Sita's life wherein; her heart boat gets sailed. The first fortnight is the bright side of Sita's life-coin. During this fortnight, only the spring sprangs in Sita's autumn-life. On the first day of the new Moon, the Moon was sighted. During the second fortnight of this very month, the Sita's life-kite flying in the vast sky, fell into the ground and made her powerless in every aspect. That's why the day of 15th August is the heart-breaking day for Sita.

Her soul gets deeply hurt. after the flag-hoisting on the Independence Day when Sita addresses her school family and reminds the school children that the Independence Day is the best festival. Our Mother-India got independence from the century old slavery today. This day is worth-writing in the golden letters in our history. This day is the result of sacrifices of our Father of Nation Mahatama Gandhi and the numerous unsung young men.

During this time only, the images of many accursed unsung martyrs get emerged in her imagination and start crying (Chilla-Chilla kar kahti hai) like this: "Why don't you tell Sita? Oh! Sita let the other martyrs remain unsung, but at least your own unsung Martyr Nath's sacrifices ought to be sung............" There is no mention of those who sacrificed their lives during 1947 INDO-PAK partition. Those unsung heroes were lying on the floors like insects and the people were crushing them under their feets. Did they get asleep themselves? Did they die without sword (TALWAR or KHARAG) or barrel? Sita say, at least once that, you're also one of the victims of the massacre of 1947. In the same war of freedom, I too lost the shine of my vermilion and became the widow". But Sita had to be quiet; keeping in view her designation of the Principal, place and the occasion of the Independence Day.

During the Monsoon month of August, the Grand-mom 'Sita' on terrace was experiencing an extraordinary pleasure by watching nature's beauty: the sun-rays were filtering through the dense tree-leaves with the kissing breeze. By beholding the nature's creation, she experienced the undefined pleasure. The grandson and granddaughter, sitting nearby her, were enjoying playing with their dolls. The sister (Granddaughter) was busy in arranging the kitchen and garments for her male & female dolls. She was giving the list of items to be purchased from the market to her brother (Grandson). By watching this play of grandchildren; the sitting nearby Grandmom became so happy that she went back to her childhood when she used to sit in the lap of her Grandmom. Sita, who lived the 40 years of her acclimatized deserted life; started wandering in the virtual life of pleasure.

The Grandmom was happy to recall her childhood memories of listening dusk songs and dawn recitals " Get up lord Krishna- your mother Yashoda has come to wake you up" (Jago Re- Krishna, Yashoda jagane aiyee) along with the love and affection of her mother. Sita also got lot of love and affection of her Paternal-Aunty (Tai Maa). The Paternal-Aunty (Tai Maa) used to narrate the story of the Bird and Crow (CHIDIYA & KAUVA) to Sita before she goes to sleep by kissing her hair. She, Paternal-Aunty (Tai

Maa) used to be overwhelmed with pleasure by the mere thought of seeing her daughter as a bride. Indeed the Paternal-Aunty (Tai Maa) was like a Goddess. She became widow at the age of 14. Just after one year of her bridalhood, she lost the shine of her vermilion (an icon of marriedhood). But, the life of this denunciative ascetic lady was indulged in the happiness and the prosperity of the children of her husband's younger brother's wife. Sita also experienced the extraordinary pleasure of being in the lap of her mother. She also had milk under the motherly veil of affection of her mother right till the age of eight years .This itself was a rare blessing to her (Sita) which only a few are lucky to have.

By having swam in the ocean of the childhood memories; Sita born in Punjab- her birth place. The beautiful Punjab is incomparable to any state of country. The beautiful fields, full of wheat, paddy, fruits, greenery and enriched with milk, butter; the lovely Punjab whose soil is full of zeal, valour, and victory. Now at her birthplace with her childhood friend Shanti, Sita started playing and reciting, "the turban of my brother is adorned with golden wreath" ("Kikli kalirdi pag mere veer di). Faster than light, the mind of Sita starts flying over the deserts of Khanewal-Multan (now in Pakistan) watching the forming & deforming sandunes, the camel ride, and the cotton fields. She (Sita) got lost in the carefree childhood memories and the unpolluted environment of her grandmaternal. About four miles away from her city, there was a beautiful village "Sioki". The grandmaternal were landlords. She starts recalling the days of her vacational stays with her (Sita) grandmaternal aunt- Krishana, Kailash- maternal uncle and her most beloved friend and sister- Raj; the daughter of her maternal aunt (Mausi) –after all they both together used to play, chat, eat musk-melon (Khabooja) wandering in the paddy fields. The simple environment of her grandmaternal; simple people with simple living amalgamated with selfless love and affection of her grandmaternal (Nana's), were the sweetest memories of her childhood and the days of adolescence. Ye, grandmaternal's house had four wells, three gardens with all varieties of flowers and the shopping centre, full of daily amenities & for the ride there were horsecarts (Tanga).

What were the days when we (Raj & Sita) used to jump in clusters of water-ponds near the wells, swinging on swing tied with trees & having cheerfully persuade the maternal aunt and with the excuse of plucking the mustard-leaves ,and then, their swing to the tree- tied swings with the pretends; chewing the sugar-canes and return home with mustard leaves and then, get scolded with love, by the maternal aunt (mother's sister).

Sita's mother's name was "Parvati" and maternal aunt's (Mausi) name was "Jamuna". At their maternal home they were called by their nick-names "Paro and Jamuna". The children of Jamuna and Paro were presumed be the toys for every inhabitant of the very entire village. For the children too, the unpolluted atmosphere in the village with cool breeze used to be much more comfortable than the crowded, suffocating atmosphere of cities. Ah! What were the days when with maternal aunt (Mami) 'Cheema', the cotton flower used to be plucked by us from the fields without the knowledge of our parents, and then, threatening by Krishna aunt (Mausi) for lodging complaint against us followed by luncheon began at aunt' s place.

But, there was hardly any reaction of the complaint made by Krishna aunt from the side of our dear moms. During those days, even the moms were helpless to scold us as we children were lucky to have a lot of love and patting from our grandmaternal parents. Our moms too would not express their intimacy towards us at our maternal' s house. One day our maternal uncle (Mama) Kailash climbed the tree to pluck mangoes in our garden & underneath the mango tree, we both sisters (Raj & Sita) alongwith aunt Krishna (mother's sister) used to pick up the mangoes. We all being in the same age group; there was hardly any difference between niece and the maternal uncle (Mama). The moment Sita & Raj arrive at grandmaternal house; the maternal uncle Kailash and aunt Krishna too used to be like free-lancer (Bindas) ,carefree personnel. The village folks were very simple, straight forward, far away from the glamour, pomp and show of the city life. It used to be fun to run away like a thief into the cotton fields alongwith the beautiful female flower-pickers and alike them only, to pick up the cotton flowers & put in the haversack made out of crochet tied on the back. Lo! one day suddenly when our elder maternal uncle (Bade Mama),while passing through the cotton fields, watched us in young maiden doing all these mischievous acts; then on return to home he gave a good doze to the ladies at home by scolding them that why they had taken very tender girls out into the fields in the hot sun? We both the sisters enjoyed this scene very much as we ourselves had gone to cotton fields without their knowledge and these poor house-wives were being scolded by our eldest maternal uncle. Ha, what was a pleasure, we both sisters were smiling on this very success of ours.

By recalling all these memories, the grandmom Sita went so deep into her past that the memories of those happy go-lucky days changed her present days of distress and melancholy into full of life and she got an inspiration from her inner-self that why these pleasant sweet memories should not be made immortal through her pen.

Coming out from her childhood memories, Sita got lost into the sweet memories of her young age. She started wandering in her childhood dreams amalgamated with quanta of imaginations of happy life. As a matter of fact, this was the beginning of reality of her younghood dreams.

This phase of life is a real image of ambitious dreams in every being whether animate or inanimate. The nature too blesses the boon of younghood with full of zeal, tenderness and beauty .

Four and half decade before, moment a girl grew to the age of 14-15 years, the then society had only one aim of getting her married. There used to be no consideration as regards the progress and achievements of a girl child in her walk-of-life. Only marriage of her was considered to be the biggest achievement in her life. The outlook and attitude of the girl was obviously used to be commensurate with the time of the then era. This unique boon of marriage also embraced Sita. But, she had one more rider with this very boon that her paternal grandmother (Dadi) was very keen to see the marriage-party of grand daughter at her residence. She (Dadi) was keen to see the holy-oblation (Kanyadan) of grand daughter at her home. Apart from the thrill of grand daughter's marriage ceremony, she (Dadi) did have an orthodox idea that as in her house, from the last four generations the holy oblation of daughter (Kanyadan) had not taken place, hence, such a house was equivalent to the hell. Even such families do not prosper in

future. From last four to five generations, the family was
not blessed with a girl child (daughter). Parvati Mom too
had given birth to three sons. The paternal-grandmom
(Dadi) had the obvious apprehensions that if, she is not
blessed with the grand- girl child (Poti) then she would be
bound to get done the holy-oblations (Kanyadan) of two of
the adopted Brahmin-girls, (Brahmin is a priestly cast in
Hindus) through her daughter-in-law 'Paro'. Ye, At last,
after a gap of 8 years the great- grandmom (Dadi) family
was blessed with a girl child and everybody in the family
out of love and affection started calling her by the name of
"SITA" (Sita was wife of lord Rama in the Hindu Epic-
"Ramayana"). Ye, now long coveted solemn desire of
marriage of the grand daughter of the grandmom (Dadi)
had to be fulfilled at the age of fourteen only. She always
considered the marriage at the age of fourteen was a sacred
deed (Punya). this desire of hers (Dadi) too got fulfilled
when Sita completed her seventeenth year.

3

Sita's maternal aunt (Mausi) used to live in Jammu. The cousin father-in-law (Chachia Sasur) of her maternal aunt (Mausi) lived in Lahore (now in Pakistan). The cousin mother-in-law (Chachi-Sas) died four to five years ago. They had two sons and three daughters. The eldest son 'Bhaskar' nick named 'Nath' at home, was of 20 years of age. The younger son was about 14-15 years old and the three daughters were in the age group of 18, 6 & 4 years. The cousin- father- in- law (Chacha Sasur) came to Jammu for visiting 'Vaishno Devi' shrine (A Hindu temple of Goddess Vaishno in the hills of Jammu-Kashmir 'Peer-Panjal Ranges') and stayed with his daughter-in-law's maternal aunt (Sita's Maternal Aunt). The cousin father-in-Law; having observed the great hospitality of his daughter–in–law, narrated his family's compulsions and proposed for the marriage of his elder son Nath. He was well conversant with the family of his daughter-in-law (Sita's maternal aunt) and always wanted a noble and decent girl like her for his son Nath. Nath after having passed his intermediate exam in the first division had also successfully completed the Railway Services Station Master's exam in the same year. Nath's father had good approach in the Railway Department. The British officials were highly impressed with his (Nath's father) personality. He got his son positioned temporarily as a TTE (Train Ticket Examiner) at 'Changa Manga' Railway station in the Lahore division (now in Pakistan).

The father himself had been at very high position in the Department of Railways in the Lahore Division. He had taken voluntary retirement from the services due to his ill-health. He had left marks of his smiling nature, sincerity, dedication to duty, and professionalism on his the then British Officials. Keeping in view the problems at home, he (Nath's father) got compelled to get his son married, at the earliest as there was nobody to look after his two very young daughters (6 & 4 years old) and the grown up daughter of 18 years age. He himself was ailing fast due to persistent illness.

The maternal aunt (Mausi) of Sita was already impressed with the personality of his younger brother-in-law (Devar) Nath. Apart from the dynamic and the pleasing personality, the Almighty had blessed "Nath" with very sweet and charming nature. He had the capacity to impress the people with his rare art of effective communication. He was a total personality in himself with his simple nature and professionalism.

The matrimonial attention of the maternal aunt (Mausi) got focussed on her own sister –Parvati's daughter-Sita.

At the earliest occasion, the maternal aunt (Mausi) visited her sister & brother-in-law's (Behan- Bahnoi) residence in Sialkot to initiate the matrimonial dialogue. Sita's mother got fully satisfied and convinced with Nath's personality after having heard from her own affectionate sister. Sita's father satisfied himself by matching the horoscopes. Sita's mother had only one reservation on the back of her mind that her care-free, lovely young daughter would have to take up the complete responsibility of the Nath's family. She (Parvati) always felt the heavenly absence of would be mother-in-law (Sas) of her daughter. But, Sita's father was determined to get this engagement go ahead after having confirmed the perfect-matching of both horoscopes under the blessings of the super-planets. Ye, the great grandmom(Dadi maa) got her long coveted desire of grand daughter's marriage fulfilled, because as such she was in great hurry to get the grand daughter married. She (Dadi) was of firm belief that if, she did not see holy daughter oblation (Kanyadan) at home, then she would never get eternal peace after her death. So, after having seen the auspicious day and as per the family customs and traditions the engagement ceremony took place. After the authentication of the matrimonial engagement, the younger brother-in-law (Devar); the resident of Lahore, Nath aimed to go to Jammu. By accompanying his sister-in-law (Bhabhi) to Jammu, Nath, was anxious to know about his fiancee Sita from his cousins (Children of his sister-in-law 'bhabhi') – specially from Raj, the daughter of Bhabhi who not only being cousin to Sita but, was an ideal friend too. Whenever Nath & Raj sat together, they always talked about Sita. Thus, Nath got fairly good idea about Sita's nature and her looks. Nath used to show a lot of interest in listening about his fiancee Sita from his own niece. On the other hand, Raj too was keen to get conversant with ideas and the nature of her uncle, so that she can render more and more information about Nath to Sita. During the summer vacation, Raj was to go to her maternal-grandparents (Nanihal) where Sita too was scheduled to reach. Nath had a very keen desire to see his fiancee, the same he got conveyed to father through his elder sister but got the negative response at this. His father asked, "why are you worried when your own sister-in-law (Bhabhi) had taken this very responsibility?" Also, those days there was no such custom to get the looks of one's fiancée in the villages of Punjab. Ye, Nath pacified himself by the idea that he is now bound to honour the decision of his sister-in-law (Bhabhi) through out the life.

"With whom one's hearts meets , then hold her hand only and whomsoever hand is held then to live with her only, unto death" ("Jide mile dil, odi bahan phadiye, jidi bahan fadiyan ode naal marna"). Ye, this song one has to sing throughout his life. Nath's sister-in-law (Bhabhi) used to get thrilled in heart by listening lofty dreams of her

younger brother-in-law (Devar). She had confidence that Nath would make Sita's married life very comfortable. She was well acquainted with the nature of both. She also had the confidence that there was very less probability of misunderstanding of any kind in future when the new relations got established within the family.

4

Now the two cities Lahore and Sialkot had developed very close ties. Both the sisters progressed matrimonial talks. Raj often used to be in search of an opportunity to tease (Chhedkhani) her friend Sita and tell more and more about Nath. After having known, about her fiancé Nath from sister Raj, Sita started dreaming about the prospective new turn of her life. With pleasant and passionate marriage conversation, Sita started swinging in the swing of passionate imagination (Kalpana ki peeng mein jhoolne). By thinking more about her future life partner; the tender heart of Sita used to rejoice. She always felt happy to know about smiling, joyful nature of the very handsome Raj's uncle, residing in Paris like city of Punjab-Lahore. When she heard positive about her, amalgamated with lofty-lofty plans, her heart not only got amused but, the feeling of fear too got aroused.

"See, Raj your sister should not be fatty (obese) ; does she look like an uneducated village girl (Jatti)? Would she be matching with your handsome smart uncle?" – used to be fun chats of Nath with her niece Raj. By all this, Sita used to feel more scary than becoming happier.

Very important point was being put by Nath's father that he was getting Nath married under compulsion, merely at the age of twenty. I am getting marriage of my able son solemnized; just to get my other children be taken of care well, amalgamated with mother-like affection and love. This thought did tie Sita in the chain of responsibilities. The pleasure and passion got replaced with future thoughts and plans. Although, these were the facts of life but, it was not easy for Sita to take up these family challenges at very young age. Raj's talks about these future responsibilities made Sita more responsible and she started realizing her duties in advance by leaving behind the care-free life of youthhood and started reciting the "Gita" (A Hindu Epic which emphasises more and more on duty without expecting the results) as regards to her duties and responsibilities of prospective married life.

5

On 27 November (1945), at the auspicious time in the
night of Tuesday the marriage of Sita-Nath got
solemnized. The marriage party arrived in the most
wonderfully adorned home of bride. The marriage pavilion
was unique & beautifully decorated. There was a big lawn
in front of Sita's house. Behind this lawn there were two
rooms for the cows. The paternal-grandmom of Sita had
firm belief that the cows are very holy and auspicious. For
her it was religious to keep cow at home; specially, to see
the cow in morning, serve the cow, feed the cow and worship
the cow. In the same sprawling lush green lawn; there was
a colorful one side open tent like canopy. The table, chairs,
and sofas were beautifully arranged to welcome the
marriage party for the feast. The tented canopy was
beautifully decorated with buntings, flowers, glittering lights,
chandeliers, flower pots with full of blooming beautiful
flowers and attractive light fountains. After all the most
lovable and favourite sister of brothers, was getting married.
The brothers along with their friends were not leaving any
stone unturned to make the pavilion the most attractive,
beautiful, unique and comfortable. The main-gate of the
pavilion had two auspicious silver pitchers (Kalash) with
beautiful rose petals and variety of eye-catching flowers.

On one of the big dias made of wooden planks, the
maternal and paternal uncles (Mama & Chacha) of Sita
alongwith their friends were sitting and supervising keenly
all the marriage arrangements of her most affectionate

niece. They were really enjoying this rare family occasion. The elder mom (Tai maa) and Parvati mom were thanking the Almighty with great happiness and the feeling of gratefulness. But, at the same time there was a thought of their daughter's adieu from their house to her own new home of wedded life. Very often their eyes would get wet with tears due to the anguish of separation of their beloved daughter. The beloved daughter who never got-off from their sight ever for a moment; was now departing from them forever.

At about 08:00 PM, the ma rriage party arrived with lot of pomp and show. The members of the marriage party (Barat) were dancing, singing and jumping in joy in front of the marriage marques. The bride-groom (Dulah) was riding the decorated mare. The mare was covered with beautiful silvery silken sheet. The bride-groom had a nuptial headwear made of flowers and tightened over the silvery headgear. Ha! he was looking very-very handsome and attractive. The fireworks were making the sky glittering. The beautiful ladies were singing the auspicious songs and eulogistic verses with the silver-pitcher on their heads. As per the prevailing customs and traditions the beautiful women were cracking jokes mingled with alleges. Although, the elderly persons were restraining the ladies to do so— but, who was bothered about them. They believed that such occasions are God gifted and hence were reciting joyfully the Punjabi marriage rhyme 'In the black pitchers, there is a cooled leafy vegetable of mustard seed and thus, there is a black pimple on the face of the groom' (*Kali-Kali kunni vich sarson ka saag, munde de muh te maata de daag hain*) "You are not at all of our choice oh ugly guy" (Sadi pasAnd the bain ve nirlojjaya tuhan nahin)

Some were reciting welcome songs, standing with flower garlands. As per the customs, the father of bride, maternal and paternal uncles, brothers were expressing their feeling of happiness, thankfulness by extending warm welcome to each and every member of marriage party. The marriage got solemnized by reciting the religious songs & prayers to the great Almighty by sitting in front of the sacred fire.

The mother along with father did holy-oblation of an amulet (the bracelet put on the bride at the time of marriage). The brothers showered the blessings on the wedded couple by throwing the flowers and eatable made of rice over their beloved sister and brother-in-law. The maternal uncle and aunty did oblation of an amulet followed by holy-donation of jewellry (Gulian) by the paternal aunt -uncle. The paternal grandmom (Dadi) was enjoying this very scene very much and thanking the great Almighty. The father was wiping the auspicious tears with his shoulder napkin. But the eyes of beloved mother were flowing with non-stop tears of happiness and she was unable to wipe them off. What an irony of the fate that the part of one's heart and soul; which is nourished with all over the years is just donated to the unknown hand and the unknown family forever. What a typical custom of our society!

The time of auspicious adieu to daughter arrived. The house in which Sita spent her memorable childhood along with friends like Shanti, Vidya and did adorn the house with dolls in her adolescence was being left forever as if, her own house is going to be of the others forever. By becoming the bonafide husband, Nath got the right on beautiful Sita Awasthi; adorned as a bride by her friends, playmates & maternal aunties. Now it was up to Nath that in what way he treats Sita; whether embraces her as his holy life-partner or treats her as one of the shoe in his feet.

The beauty of Sita was beyond words and imagination. The play-mates and friends had adorned her hands and feet with scented, colourful henna. They had adorned her with variety of beautiful garments and beautiful aids. There were beautiful leistering sets of ivory-amulet with golden-jewellery of designer's choice on her beautiful forearms. Both the hands were woven with beautiful silver-pebbles, chained in silver strings. The beautiful dot (Bindi) on her beautiful forehead with the designer's nose–ring; leistering designer's suit, full of silver- golden wreaths, flowery designs along with shining, scarf was meant to cover the head in order to form a veil-known as "Jhimmi" during that era, was adding lot to the unique, natural God-gifted serene beauty of Sita.

The holy vermilion in the hair parting (symbol of Indian women's happy state of enjoying covertures) put by her husband at the time of marriage, in presence of the sacred fire, swearing by the name of God, as an auspicious symbol of a married lady, was shining in beautifully dressed block curly hair of the bride. This holy vermillion as symbol of an Indian women's happy state of enjoying covertures is considered to be an icon of women's prestige and grand respect in the society. This is the sign of the great personality of women and her women-hood. What to talk about mortals even the immortals can not take her granted for any mischief.

This vermilion is a covertures flag which is awarded by the husband of a lady as an icon of wedded life. The beautifully adorned bride in the attire of married woman; was being bid farewell by her beloved brother with wet eyes of happy tears. Their own affectionate lovely sister to whom they (brothers) had ever loved, enjoyed watching her growing from adolescence to younghood; was now going to be of somebody else's forever. The brother brought their sister by carrying her in beautiful palanquin on their shoulders to the bus–stop where the other members of the marriage party(Barat) were awaiting eagerly to take the bride along with them. At the time of auspicious-adieu; Sita and all her kith and kins were sobbing, weeping with soaked eyes of pleasant tears. The farewell meeting of mother and daughter flew in the streams of tears and its reflection adorned Sita's face with glitter and charm amalgamated with appearance of forthcoming responsibility and challenges of new life mixed with the sweet memories of her parents and maternal home.

⊘⊘⊘

6

Nath was extremely happy by the thought of achieving the new height of the new destination of his life. His friends were enjoying and expressing their joy by showering their best wishes with wishful comments for Nath with Sita's happy married life. By the smile of Nath ;it was quite evident that he was very relaxed and contented after having come out of the last six months' dilemma.

The newly married bride Sita; too was awaiting to cover new path of her journey with hope and confidence of golden era. Which spinster will not feel proud and lucky for having got the most handsome husband like Nath? The only difference in the bride's thinking was that, while Nath was engrossed in the pleasant dreams of his new life; Sita alongwith her pleasant dreams, had great sense of her forthcoming family responsibilities. On one hand, she enjoyed the pleasure of married life and on the other hand a feeling always arose of being awarded the designation of "Mom" of the three children (Nath's sisters) and stepping into the adulthood at very young age. Most of the people enjoyed passing the taunting remarks on her designated title of 'Mom'. But, how Sita could forget that she was one of the branch of the big banyan like family tree with full of affection and the sense of duty. One phase of Sita's life spent under the parental love and affection with the achievements; had stepped into the phase of life filled with dedication, penance and responsibilities at in-laws' place.

The close and dear friend of Sita; who was fully aware of the internal feelings of her friend, and was pretending to forget that all. With the mixed feelings in heart and soul; Sita stepped into her permanent new home at Ramgali' Lahore on the 28th day of November 1945.

At her in-laws' place; in place of the mother-in-law, the grand-maternal-mother-in-law (Nani Saas) was standing to welcome Sita with auspiciously filled silver-pitchers, garlands as per the then prevailing customs and tradition of Punjab. The absence of her heavenly abode daughter (Naths's mother) at this very auspicious occasion was being deeply felt. With the child like naivety the simple, innocent three small girls, out of which two were of tender age; embraced their dear newly-wedded sister-in-law (Bhabi).

The beautiful ladies were eagerly enjoying and watching the veil-beauty (Ghoonghat) of the bride and showering the blessings with auspicious gifts. Abruptly, Nath's dad (Babuji) with heavy voice mingled with sorrows and happiness acclaimed 'Rakhkho' (nick name of Nath's maternal-grand mother, i.e. mother of Nath's mother) "Lo, see, who has come to your house?"

By holding the hands of the two tender girls (Nath's younger sisters aged 4 & 6 years); along with the household keys (*The keys of lockers, household boxes are handed over to the eldest bride (daughter-in-law) as the symbol of passing the family responsibilities as per the Indian traditions*); the old man (Nath's father–Babuji) put them into the lap of Sita and said, "My dear daughter (BETI) this is the property of your heavenly abode mother-in-law". Sita saw the reality of her thoughts of attaining the adulthood at very young age.

What she thought of that–she got the title of "mom" on the first day of marriage. The house was full of guests. Each and every person was begging Sita to shower the motherly affections on three young girls who had lost their own mother at very young age. Some of the women were also telling in between that, if you keep these girls with a lot of love and affection, then not only you will be truthful to the Almighty but, also to the society (Pyar nal rakengi te rab kolon wi te jag kolon wi sachi Rahengi).

The auspicious ivory bracelet (Kangan) were opened to play the folk-marriage games between the bride and bride-groom for the fun's sake. The fun-game of Punjab continued with the declaration of lose & win. During the play, when Nath could not pick the ivory-bracelet and lost the game, then one of the beautiful lady out of the crowd leered "Oh you got defeated now itself, then how will you dominate her in future? Ye! these three poor girls (Nath's sister) have lost their luck." Sita's heart got into pieces with the sarcastic derogatory remarks of the guest-lady. The apprehensions that she (Sita) had in her mind about the prevailing sick ideology of the then society came in front of her eyes and obviously she got upset.

The cousin sister of Nath, who was very intelligent and visionary immediately countered the lady's remarks by saying, "Sita herself is a child and this is the age of her playing, enjoying, and not of shouldering such great responsibilities & this very thrusted Motherhood." These very affectionate words of hers were sufficient enough to encourage Sita to face the future challenges.

Now for Sita, going to her own maternal home was just a formality and hardly any scope of there to stay overnight due to the motherly duties at her in-laws place. One day most affectionately 'Babuji' said to Sita "My dear daughter, please open the almirah and the boxes so that I may too see the property of your heavenly abode mother-in-law."

While opening of the ancestral boxes, Sita's heart got emotionally filled with joy by observing the deep love and affection of the great mother who had kept all these for her would be daughter-in-law with the hope of gifting. The mother who had collected all these beautiful ornaments, with the golden-dreams of gifting the same, but the irony of fate, did not bless her with an opportunity to gift these items with her own hands to her daughter-in-law. Inside the two boxes, she had kept the two sets of gold-ornaments, separately in each of the box along with other items for her two would be daughter-in-laws (one for Nath's bride & the other his younger brother Krishan's bride). Ah! the great affection of the father-in-law (Babuji) and the dream box of the heavenly abode mother-in-law; made Sita's heart topped up with kindness and this too turned the life of Sita totally to face happily the challenge of the new life and compelled her always to remain contended and happy in the world of responsibilities. Thus, 2-3 months passed by in Lahore. Nath was posted at nearby railway station 'Changa-Manga' and used to do daily up and down.

7

To celebrate' Lohri festival (A festival of Punjab, which is celebrated on the eve of setting of winter season by sitting around the bonfire with relatives and friends and chewing the seasonal dry-fruits, viz. cashew nuts, groundnuts, almonds, Jiggery mixed with mustard seeds. Paro Mom sent lot of dry-fruits, foodstuff alongwith the few gifts to her beloved daughter through her brother with a request to Sita's father-in-law (Babuji) to allow her to visit her maternal for a week or so. Lo, Sita after having got the permission; alongwith her brother on the same day, arrived at parents' house where each and every member of the family was awaiting. Sita met her childhood day's friends. One of her friends got married on the same day, the day Sita had married.

Sita did met her in Lahore when she had come with her husband; from her remote village, to visit the big and beautiful city Lahore after their marriage. She narrated the pleasant memories of their Lahore visit. Ye, Sita wondered that she being in Lahore had seen nothing of the beautiful city except the place of her in-laws. She felt as if something is missing in her life. For a moment she became uncomfortable.

There was lot of happiness and joy at Sita's mother place due to her arrival in the festive season. After having got their daughter with them, the parents felt as if, they have been blessed with the treasure of love and prosperity. Ye, just after three days, Nath (Sita's Husband) reached her place to get her back to Lahore as his Father (Babuji) was ailing. There was no choice left for Sita except accompanying Nath back to the place of her in-laws. The memorable three days spent at mother's place brought Sita back to her childhood days. After having witnessed kiddish, Sita's this very carefree childhood naivety, full of joy, her friend Vidya felt as if her friend Sita, has turned to be more playful after marriage.

Moment they (Nath & Sita) alighted the horse-cart (Tanga); Nath revealed that 'Babuji' (Nath's father) is not at all sick and his sickness was just an excuse to get Sita back home as everybody feeling lonely at home and he too was missing her badly. No doubt, Sita got depressed and felt uneasy. But, on arrival of her in-laws place; Babuji (Nath's Father) uttered these emotional words, " My beloved daughter (Beti), this is the great injustice to you and to your parents who have only daughter and she too is not being allowed to stay longer there even during the festive season; obviously, makes everybody sad these at home. Also, here too you are within the four walls and hardly get any time for yourself. But, I am totally helpless as these three kids of mine had missed you so much in the last four days that they never missed their own heavenly abode mother." These kind utterances of his; full of love and helplessness, brought Sita back to the days of daughter-in-law amalgamated with the very family commitments.

These affectionate words of her 'Babuji' (Father-in-law) gave immense pleasure to Sita and made her proud that she is most lovable and demanding to her own family. The younger daughter of Nath's aunty used to visit quite often to provide her motivational guidance to run the house efficiently and in orderly manner. Having lost her mother in the childhood, she stayed most at her maternal uncle place. Her marriage too was solemnized by 'Babuji' (Nath's Father) and she was most lovable sister to Nath. Nath had lots of regard for this very sister. She started getting sympathized with Sita after having watched her being awful busy with the childish husband's sister (Nanad) & in the household, daytoday affairs. On her (Nanad's) recommendation, Nath's aunty directed him to accompany Sita to famous shopping complex 'Anarkali' in Lahore.

Nath was astonishingly amused; as he too was passing his younghood days, by subduing his ambitions, pleasures, leisure of the newly wedded life under the prevailing dull environment at home resulted due to the sudden demise of his mother at early age. This pleasant offer of outing with his darling wife obviously was a great sign of relief to Nath in the same fashion as the aged parents of young siblings keep waiting for their children to attain adulthood. The younger sister, after the unprecedented death of Mom, used to cry the whole day and had become very cranky in nature. The younger brother Krishana was 12-13 years old and was naughty. He too was to be tempted with gifts to get him persuaded to be at home.

After having persuaded, loading youngsters with the gifts; the first time Nath & Sita were lucky to have an outing of their own. The 3 hours memorable time spent together in the cinema theatre was a rare boon to Sita & Nath from their beloved dad (Babuji). On their return to home the pleasant memories of those three hours got replaced with the feeling of self-guilt on hearing the painful cry and sign of their ailing beloved dad (Babuji).

Out of the three-four months stay in Lahore; there were merely two occasions when Nath & Sita had an opportunity to be together on outings. The second time, when they had an outing to watch a romantic movie 'Heer-Ranjha' (Punjabi movie based on Romeo & Juliet story); the younger naughty brother Krishna got made an entry in the cinema theatre and saw his brother and Sister-in-law (Bhaiya & Bhabhi) sitting there together & even half of the movie was not yet over that he yelled amusingly, "Oh, I see, you people are sitting together here". "I am going to tell our dad (Babuji). He was tremendously happy on his smart act of catching us sitting together in the cinema. Krishna had irresistible proclivity for spicy dishes (Chaat) and was very fond of eating. After having come out of the cinema hall; Nath said to his brother, "Krishna very delicious spicy dishes (Chaat) are available, would you care for that?"

What else Krishna wanted more; so abruptly he announced, "Well I am not going to tell our dad regarding your watching movie provided you people do not tell about my munching of spicy delights' (Chaat). Having heard this very amusing Krishna's agreement amalgamated with simplicity & regards, made both Sita & Nath to have a hearty laugh. Sita's sister-in-law (Nanad) i.e. elder sister of Nath was of contemporary to Nath in age and used to be very happy in every way but, quite reluctant to take care of her younger brother & sisters. This responsibility too was solely of Sita.

8

After 4-5 months, Nath's father (Babuji) decided to shift 'Changa-Manga' because it was too tiring for Nath to commute everyday. After having locked the 'Ram Gali' house, Lahore; all landed up in 'Changa-Manga'. Although, the railway station was small but equipped with beautiful environment around the house. It was a treasure house for oranges, citreous fruits, milk and milk-cakes. Quite often, people used to drink milk and curd after having mixed with milk-cake. All other staff members of the railway station were very simple and of mixing nature. Hence, we did not feel to be stranger there. In the neighbourhood. there was a muslim family of Mr. Attaullah Butt and his wife named Kalsoom Begum (*Begum is an Urdu word meaning wife*). They had two lovely sons. There was a common wall between the houses of Sita and Kalsoom Begum. Very soon both families became very close friends and Sita after having met Kalsoom felt as if, she has met either to her childhood days friend or an elderly sister. Babuji (Nath's father) used to enjoy quite often the happy meetings, chit-chat, of these two sisters standing beside their common wall. He was contended to see that his daughter-in-law was getting love and affection of an elderly & matured lady at home. In the evening, both the families quite often sat together and Babuji (Nath's father) entertained all of us by copying the accents and speaking of broken Hindi by the British officials.

Thus, in this fashion our time was being passed very happily. Sita had come out of her maiden days of fun and ferry, joy, play and kiddish nature. She had now turned to be a matured lady-wife and her happiness lay in the happiness of her family. Having blessed at home with affection of Babuji (Father-in-law); love of her husband, Sita started experiencing all the comforts and joys at her small house in that small village. Kalssom Begum had become 'Kalssoom Aapa' ('Aapa' *is an Urdu word meaning elder sister*) to everybody at home. She was a great well-wisher to Sita. One day Kalsoom Aapa said abruptly to Sita, "You are looking tired, restless, and weak. This was true indeed from the last few days, Sita was too feeling weak and lazy but, was unable to find out the cause. Kalsoom Aapa was an experienced lady and after having guessed the prospective motherhood; she during chat hinted Babuji (Nath's Father) to send Sita with Nath to a lady doctor for the check-up. Immediately, babuji' directed Nath to accompany Sita to Lahore for medical check-up. The innocent Sita was not able to understand her disease and why she was being taken to doctor. Nath got an excuse to have tour to Lahore alongwith the pretence of showing Sita to a doctor. On reaching Lahore, they visited first to a lady-doctor. After having known the ailment of Sita, Nath jumped with joy to the top of ladder since, a symbol of their intimate-eternal love was going to shine in their family awarding them a happy parenthood.

Enroute Lahore-'Changa-Manga'; Sita and Nath were rejoicing with gratefulness to the Almighty for this very rare gift of their prospective parenthood. Spontaneously with rejoice Nath uttered, "Now Nath Bhaskar's house would be illuminated by his 'Bhanu' (name given to his prospective child). They took two hours to reach home. The happiness spread all over the house with this very happy news. Babuji's happiness was beyond imagination. On the second day itself, the maternal grandmother of Nath (Nani) was recalled so that, there is an experienced lady to take care of Sita at this very stage. Ye, this poor 'Nani' (mother of Nath's mother) had nothing except a daughter who too got heavenly abode at very early age.

During the month of June, the marriage of the eldest sister-in-law (Nanad) of Sita was solemnized in the famous historical city 'Gujranwala' of the Punjab. Although, now there were no limits of Babuji's happiness but, the workload had increased at home after having bid farewell to the eldest sister-in-law (Nanad). The ailing father-in-law, aged maternal-grandmother (Nani) and her own health due to pregnancy-sickness was a challenge for Sita in itself. Having watched all this as well as the hair-combing and dressing of the two young sister-in-laws (Nanad), Kalsoom Aapa used to feel pity and with the heavy heart would acclaim that perhaps the world of happiness of this young bride lies in the happiness of this very family.

Keeping in view Sita's condition ; Babuji (Nath's father) had appointed an attendant named Mohan. He was able to perform light –house-jobs and handle the youngest girl (Nanad), who was stubborn (Ziddi) in nature. Babuji's long coveted desire of taking his grandson into his lap and play got fulfilled. In August, 1946 just on hearing the pleasant word grandson (Pota); Babuji thanked the great Almighty and offered prayers to his ancestors and the family idols-God Saindas –with wet eyes full of tears as he did remember our Heavenly abode paternal-grandmom (Dadi-Babuji's late wife). Krishna got mad with this very happy news and went running to the railway station to convey to his elder brother that he has became a proud uncle (Chacha) of a newly born.

In no time the inhabitant of this very small town came to know the good news and got pouring in at our home to pay their hearty congratulations. The priest (Pandit) was invited to see the horoscope of the newly born and got conducted the naming ceremony function. The function got solemnized on an auspicious day alongwith relatives and friends.

Nath had already expressed his desire to his sister that the child should be named 'Bhanu' (meaning Sun) as he himself was hesitant to express the same to his dad (Babuji) out of regards. As such the father's sister (Bhua) was supposed to baptize her nephew during those days. All the residents started addressing 'Bhanu-Bhanu' to this very icon(Chirag) of the Bhaskar family. But, Bhanu was being addressed by a number of nicknames by his grandpop (Dadaji). After a few days there was 'Rakhi-festival'(Rakhi *is a festival of sister-brother wherein, brother swears to protect his sister by getting a band of brotherhood by his sister*). Babuji too got seated with the ten days old grandson in his lap. Both his sons, daughter-in-law (Bahu) and the son-in-law (his elder daughter's husband) were sitting nearby. The old-maternal grandmother (Nani) with the sign of relief and joy was showering the thousands and thousands of blessing to 'Bhanu' in each and every breath of hers. She was also offering the prayers to the great Almighty with thanks, Nath was very busy taking photographs of his beloved son Bhanu. Bhanu was like a lovable toy for everybody.

The first 'Karva-Chauth' festival after the marriage was celebrated. (Karva-Chauth *is a festival wherein; the whole day fast is observed by the lady wife for the long life of her husband*). Mom and brothers of Sita, reached 'Changa-Manga' with a lot of gifts. As such the maternal-grandmother ('Nani'- Mother of Bhanu's mother) had not seen Bhanu earlier and Sita's mother was very anxious to visit her daughter's home. She was very much proud and delighted to observe the love and respect and appreciation earned by Sita from her family in such a short duration of time.

The love and affection of her father-in-law, the maternal-grand-mother-in-law (Nani-Saas); the blind love of her husband and the affectionate attachment of children towards her and a lovely son in her lap, made Sita's mother so happy that she knew no limits of joy. After having stayed 4-5 days at her daughter's place, she returned to her own house.

9

Time was passing at its own speed. Each and every day for Sita – Nath was festive day. Bhanu's kiddish activities, movements, smiles, and joyful shrieks had made everybody gay and busy. 'Deepawali' festive season got set in. (Deepawali— is a festival of lights celebrated by Indians with gay. Historically, this day God Rama was back to his Empire Ayodhya after defeating Ravana emperor of Sri Lanka, i.e. popularly the victory of goodness over evils). Not only was this the first 'Deepawali' after their marriage, but also the first 'Deepawali' festival of their son Bhanu. Babuji (Nath's father) expressed his joy by having distributed sweets to all the residents of 'Changa-Manga'. All the relatives and friends gifted a lot of garments and toys to lovely Bhanu. The small house of Babuji got turned into beautiful garden of colourful flowers of relatives.

The old maternal-grandmother (Nani) never got tired by expressing her contentment and lot of appreciation for Sita stating that she got her relieved from all the diseases & worries by getting her enthroned on the Royal Seat. Nath too considered himself be very lucky to have such a devoted wife like Sita. Now even Kalsoom Aapa started saying, "Sita you're great. You relinquished all your own desires; earned pleasure by dedicating yourself to the world of duties and became contented in the true sense. Actually, (God) Allah is also very happy on your deeds."

Bhanu started talking and used to talk in his childish tongue(totli-zuban). Everybody competing in the family that their names should be uttered first by Bhanu. Sita & Nath too were in the same race; whether Bhanu would utter first mom or papa (Dad).

This extreme happiness of this very short period did not last long, babuji's earnest desire to celebrate first 'Lohri' festival of his grandson did not get fulfilled. God has destined something different. A fortnight before the Lohri in the month of December, he got heavenly abode. The great shock of Babuji's death was intolerable for everybody. Nath was already deprived of his mother's love and affection and now even the blissful hand of his father too got vanished leaving him like an orphan. Losing Dad in the young age, was itself a great shock for Nath amalgamated with the responsibilities of his younger brother and sisters. They too had become orphan. The all joyful atmosphere at home got suddenly vanished. The total family responsibilities now lay on Nath.

Bhanu got hardly for a year or so, the love and affection of his own father and paternal uncle (Chacha). Sita's joyful life at 'Changa-Manga' got ended within a few months. The destiny was not ready to bless, Sita any longer with the love and affection of her babuji (Father-in-law), Kalsoom Aapa and the golden era of glitteriest younghood. In the age of mere 20 years, she lost all the happiness alongwith her beloved motherland.

1 5 August, 1947 is written in the golden letters in the history of Indian Subcontinent; and it will remain so ever incoming hundreds and hundreds of years. No doubt the dawn of 15 August glorified the forehead of Mother India. The redness of dawn made centre headline in between laid (maang) of Mother India very glittery. Although, the sons of soil were singing the National Anthem 'Jan gan man' (In everybody's soul) and 'Vande matram' (Prayers to mother land) but, at the same time lots of brides were losing their bridal vermilion (Sindoor), the families and families were vanishing and the life-lamps of homely comforts got extinguished. No doubt it's true that our country got independence due to the sacrifices of thousands and thousands of patriots and martyrs; but ,lots of Nation-lover lost their lives and many women lost their bridal vermilion. The number of mothers of the great sons like martyr Bhagat Singh, Chandrashekhar Azad lost their beloved ones & then only Mother India got rid off the slavery. One would be suffocated with agony if, the pages of history of India's Independence are turned. Although, Mother India was targeted by so many of her dear ones e.g Portuguese, French, the Greek & many more. Turkese empire ruled her too, but, the great mother remained immortal with one name, 'Mother India' .In front of the pride of the great 'Mother India', the each and every empire surrendered itself & enjoyed her motherly gifts.

Alas! a day came when the great 'Mother India' got divided into two parts in the pursuit of freedom from the

British Empire. Oh! on the eve of Independence the great undivided India (Akhand Bharat) from the time immemorial; got divided into two parts.

There was a turmoil on the night of 15 August, 1947. Changa-Manga being a small town. Nath and Sita alongwith other three families took a decision that it would be wise to shift to Lahore for a few days as there may be danger to their lives there. On 14 August at 4:00 AM, these four families inclusive of Kalsoom Aapa's family left Changa-Manga. Before leaving, Sita assured her servant Mohan that they would be back home after a few days and he must look-after the house.

Though the army was deployed fully from Changa-Manga to Lahore, but, still the brutal (haivans) militants, clad with green coloured clothes with half moon-starred badges were moving freely in groups; unchecked, uncontrolled with killing instinct and thirst of the human-blood. Ah! the men and men were thirsty of men's blood. No humanity was left. These patrons of brutality (haivans) were searching each and every house shouting the slogans, "Pakistan is only ours, ye this is our only slogan— we have got Pakistan joyously and would take over Hindustan forcibly".(Pakistan hamara hai , yehi hamara nara hai. Hans ke liya hai Pakistan, larh ke lenge Hindustan.)

The terrorized Sita, with Bhanu on her chest, was sitting in the train alongwith Kalsoom Aapa. The two husband's sisters (Nanad) were in the laps of their motherly sister-in-law (Bhabhi- wife of elder brother Nath). Krishna, Butt Saheb & other gents, were standing outside judging the situation & were pondering deeply over what would happen further after reaching Lahore? Sita was fully hopeful that on reaching Lahore, she would be able to join her family members alongwith her children; because, at that time it was much expected that Lahore is an integral part and parcel of India. Kalsoom Aapa got memorized to Nath and Sita a few confessions of Mohammedan faith (Kalma) from the holy 'Quran' (the holy book of Islam-the Muslims), so that these savage could be totally convinced that Nath, Sita and Krishna are true Muslims (The believers of Islam). As such Kalsoom Aapa had given her mantle (Burka – a sort of black gown used by Muslim women to cover their entire body leaving the eye-lit opened, as per their religious faith).

Ye on reaching Lahore, it got ascertained that Lahore had become the part of Pakistan. All got terrified after having seen the death-dance at Lahore Railway Station. There was a naked dance of cruelty and inhumanity. One could hear cries, death-cries all around and there were cries of weeping children.

The cries of helpless women with a sign of being raped by these savage, in-human characters (haivans), Sita and Nath felt impossible to reach their house at Ram Gali from the railway station and hence they decided to stay put at the Railway Station and proceed further to Jammu as it was being ruled by the Hindu King and hence, there was a great probability for peace and safety.

In the waiting room of Lahore Railway Station; Sita's family and Kalsoom Aapa were sitting. The children were instructed not to talk at all to each other as there was a great fear of being spotted as Hindu's, if the name is pronounced by them during the chat. Kalsoom Aapa, with her intelligence was facing boldly the then prevailing situations and pacifying all the time Sita, not to get afraid at all. Nath and Krishna were standing outside. The 'OM' (the symbol of Hindu deity) was inscribed on Naht's right wrist.On the advice of Butt sahib (Kalsoom Aapa's husband), Nath had covered the inscription 'OM' with a bandage so that nobody gets suspicious of his being the Hindu. The each and every moment the atmosphere was getting worst and worst with full of hatred and genocide. The happy families were becoming homeless. Everybody was worried with the thought that what would be worst further, who or nobody is going to be at his/ her destination.

Will they be at their destination or not? Everybody in their hearts were remembering their deity (God) and begging earnestly for their very survival.

Meanwhile, the train to Wazirabad arrived. Everybody did consultation and concluded that any how let us reach Wazirabad by boarding this train and from there, some how we would endeavour to reach Jammu. It was very risky to stay longer at Railway station in Lahore. Butt Saheb owned the responsibility of safety of his fast friend Nath and his family to the old man; sitting in the train compartment,. Kalsoom Aapa who had showered all her love and affection on Sita over the years; started weeping bitterly, after having embraced Sita to her heart. They both knew well that there is no possibility of their meeting again in future. The train started moving slowly on the railway-track leaving behind everything. The soil of motherland too got left behind wherein; these people took birth and grew. They had a beautiful tiny home there with lots of their future dreams. All were being left behind forever and ever. Sita had lingering agony (Kasak) but, within a moment she pacified herself and convinced her mind that this is a temporary phase and moment the situation improves we are going to be back to our sweet homes. This poor soul (Sita) did not know that in future her own country (motherland) would become a dream Nation for her. She was unable to understand the destiny. Nobody knew what course to his/her destiny had been destined by the great Almighty (God).

All the time Nath was assuring her, pacifying her that after having escorted her and the children to Jammu; he would be back for his official duty. "There you stay-put comfortably for sometime. See that the children do not face any problem. Moment the situation improves I will take leave to take you and children back to my duty place". Moment the train arrived Wazirabad the chain of thoughts of Nath & Sita fell apart, the situation was worst and miserable on that day and there was a total chaos in Wazirabad city. It was full of ghurchy and genocide.

Hundreds and hundreds of women were in miserable condition. For the sake of their modesty (Izzat) a lot of young ladies and maidens had ended their lives by jumping from the roof-top. Oh! there were half-charred dead bodies of young children, the living dead bodies who had lost their husbands and became widow. Ah! there were Moms whose babies got killed in heinous atmosphere resulted due to bloody Indo-Pak partition. It was pathetic to see the children crying & dying for the want of milk. Drinking water was hardly available as the water resources were full of blood, heads of killed people by the brute(haivans); the enemy of human race and thirsty of human's blood. Ah! perhaps even God could have felt ashamed after having witnessed this naked-dance of cruelty, human genocide but, the man was not bothered at all as it had turned to animals and started dancing nude -dance of cruelty and human genocide. Ah, how freely these cruel were moving after having adopted the devils attire.

There was no way left out to reach Jammu. The roads were damaged and railway tracks were unearthed. The telephone/ telegram lines were cut and there was hue & cry all over. All people were sitting subdued, terrified and horrified as the angels of death were moving all around. However, the three days got over in this horrified atmosphere at Wazirabad Railway Station. Since, no route was left for Jammu and hence somehow Nath & Sita headed to Sialkot and reached Sita's Mom place. Though, Mom (Sita's mother) was in Multan with her eldest son but, the rest of the members of the family had great relief after having seen their son-in-law and daughter hale and hearty as they had gone through hardships for the last three horrible days. They thanked God. for having been inside the four walls of their house as they now were unaware of the genocide taking place outside their house.

⊘⊘⊘

11

Just after two days only, both brothers were insisting to go to Changa-Manga railway station. The government declaration that all the non-muslim employees must reach Delhi, after 15 August, 1947, so that they may be issued the new posting orders; was always in their mind. Inspite of persuasion by all the family members; the two brothers left for their duty as the duty was paramount for them. They boarded the train from Sambadiyal railway station. There was a hue and cry of the passengers. The wrong-doers were also hunting for the life of the mankind. Both brothers entered into the passenger compartment and at the same time form the other door; four to five wrong doers entered the compartment; shouting/howling "Pakistan Zindabad" (Long Live Pakistan). Moment they resorted to killing of the passengers; both the brothers came out of the train from the same entry-door. Ah, both the brothers got spotted immediately by the wrong-doers and were chased by them for a good amount of time unless a Messenger of God arrived and escorted these two brothers safely to their house. Sita's Dad at home, expressed gratitude to the sacred-soul (the gentleman) and thanked the Great Almighty.

Oh! Again after two days, Nath got ready to leave as he was in a hurry to reach Delhi. Nath was confident of his intelligence and was full of zeal and youth. He (Nath) was confident to tackle each and every unseen adverse situation. The Government administration too had geared up a little bit further. Nath was amused and thrilled to reach Changa-

Manga railway station at the earliest so that he comes to know about his new posting. He (Nath) was equally curious to know the new changes having taken place in the country as well as anxious to watch the turmoil (Hulchal) and trumpets (Kolahal) of the freedom. Despite the persuasion by all the family members when Nath did not get convinced to stay-put; then Krishna too accompanied him with the pretence that it is not advisable for the brother to go alone in this turmoil and horrified atmosphere. Two are always better than one. The barber-servant, who was a Muslim, also accompanied them so that no problem of any kind is faced enroute.

The family members were very much scared with already occured two adverse events. The Paternal-Grand-Mom ; with tears in her eyes, was praying to God for their safety and welfare. Very smilingly and affectionately, Nath assured the weeping Sita and son Bhanu that after having reached Delhi in a day or two, having marked the attendance in the new office; would be back home within two-three days and take them along to India. Hence, the luggage should be kept ready during this period.

With the depressed heart Sita along with Bhanu went to a hall on the first floor; which had the window facing towards the narrow street. She was watching through the window her beloved, dedicated, duty-bound husband and praying earnestly to her God for his well-being; Sita was nervous and depressed by having faced the untoward terrorized and horrified past events enroute. She had not forgotten the horrified scene of Wazirabad railway station till date and by its mere thought she used to start shivering. Bhanu too was crying "Papa-Papa" with his tender lips and bidding farewell to Papa by waving hand as more than this he has not learned to utter. Abruptly, God knows, what thought came in Nath's mind that after having reached the narrow street, Nath returned home after a few steps; reached Sita's room and once more he embraced Bhanu with his heart looked up Sita again, wiped his tears and climbed down the stairs with heavy heart taking the steps forward.

After having watched Nath's returning home Sita's sister-in-law (Bhabhi); who was standing downstairs in the lobby was smiling to the glory. To uncertain his act, Nath pretended, Bhabhi (Sister-in-law) I left my wrist-watch in the room. Bhabhi with mysterious smile said, "Lo, see your wrist-watch is tied up on your wrist but, the watch of your heart is of course has been left behind in the room." This remark of Bhabhi (sister-in-law) was towards Sita.

Standing at the same window; Sita was awaiting for those happy moments when her beloved Nath would return home. The fire of hatred, the human killing by the wrong-doer in the adjoining villages had already reached the door of Sita's village. Everyday it used to be news that the group of notorious wrong-doer (gundas) of x-locality has butchered the people, looted (robbed) them and ran-away. It was the afternoon of the third day, all were resting after lunch in their houses, suddenly we heard a cry with grief, " I with folded hands request you to take the key of the locker, (treasury), take all the jewellery & money but spare my daughter and husband from your heinous killing."

Ah! All got quiet soon. Nothing was left; all were killed by the cruel gang. All the neighbours were shocked, grieved and stunned after having watched the sad scene of cruelty. The lobby of the same house was stained with blood and the dead bodies; which used to be at once upon a time a happy paradise, prosperous family with son & daughter. Ah! there were two dead children on the chest of dead housewife adjacent the dead body of her husband. No whereabout of the two young daughters. When the neighbours started search of the two young daughters, suddenly they heard the subdued voice of the youngest son of the same family who somehow had managed to hide himself in the clay-oven (tandoor) avoiding the sight of the killers; "Both sisters are confined in the room".

The young boy narrated the whole episode, witnessed by him through the hole of the clay-oven, to the neighbours. as the said room was opened. Alas! it was stunning and shocking to see the miserable condition of those two sweet-slain daughters, there tongue was out; the blood stains were spread all over the mouth. Their eyes were stagnant and wide open; the acid bottles were lying aside. The acid bottles are normally evasion at Godsmith's house and it was quite evident that those young sweet daughters embraced the death by swallowing the acid in order to protect their modesty. The mother of these slain-daughters was thrown into the well by the notorious wrong-doers (gundas) with the excuse that she was making hue and cry. The dead body of the poor mother too was taken out of the well. This was a heart breaking pathetic scene and everybody got stunned and horrified. Within a second the well-bred, happy family got assassinated by the gangs of wrong doers and Sita too was staring (tak-taki) with sigh. The dead body of the two sweet girls, whose slain mother, just two hours before was urging her (Sita) to find out grooms for them. Ye, she was pondering that till date, nobody could understand the destiny and will of God. Having witnessed the heart-breaking heinous scene, all the neighbours got terrified. All were of the same view that it would be good to leave this place for a few days.

The leaders of the Nation were quite concerned about the safety of the people and the camps were arranged at several places for the re-habilitation. The security arrangements were made by Government to ensure the safety of the people of villages. People have never thought of even in dreams whether these tents are temporary shelters for the safety or they are going to leave their motherland and their ancestors' houses forever. Alongwith others Sita too started getting ready to stay in the camps for a few days with her aged grandmother, paternal-grandaunt (Tai-Maa) and father, as she was awaiting Nath to come and proceed to a new place alongwith their child-Bhanu. The old paternal-grandmom (Dadi) was whole night busy in digging a hole in the ground so that the costly ornaments and gold-jewellry be hidden underneath. Everybody was hopeful that the people are bound to return to their homes after having stayed in the camps for a few days and hence, to carry gold and silver ornaments outside of the house was not worth. Some of the boxes with clothes were kept with their reliable Muslim friends.

Alas! there was a totally different policy of Government. The aim was to get all the displaced assembled at one place and carry all of them to border. Some of the people started realizing that they have to change their religion in order to stay put here (Pakistan). Some of were of the view that there is no need to change the religion during the promised rule as earlier too was Muslim empire. General public had the view that it hardly matters which Government rules them. Gradually, the savagery (haivaniyat) and killing had spread fully all over the villages, the chair of the law and order was fully occupied by the cruel and wrong-doers. Nobody ever knew that one would be a refugee and homeless (Khanabadosh). Oh! it was an awful happening of people-migration caused by change of Governments.

12

Sita sitting in the horse-cart (Tanga) alongwith her elder mother (Tai-Maa), aged paternal-grandmother (Dadima), and father-in-law (Babuji) was aheading towards a new direction; destination of which she herself even did not know. There was a long row of horse-carts on the pedestrian lane; loaded with so many families alike Sita's family with the hope that this journey of theirs is short-lived and they all are going to be back to their houses. On reaching at the refugee camp; there was a row of trucks (military-vehicles),which were being loaded with children and aged people to carry them to *Dera Baba Nanak* (a border town between India & Pakistan). The trucks were being loaded so much that it seemed as if, the animals are being loaded rather human beings; in order to transport them from one place to another. It was so suffocated that it was not possible even to breathe, nature too was torching to its extreme and was gifting the hot summer full of suffocation. During the rainy month of August, with full of humidity and piercing hot; the trucks were being loaded with hundreds and hundreds of people against its carrying capacity of fifty. Even after having got packed in the truck, Sita had thrown the box of children's garments, which she brought from her house, as she was afraid that the army personnel may not allow her to sit into the truck with the box due to the scarcity of the space. Abruptly, the truck stopped after having watched the crowd of helpless people in the village enroute. Ah! it was a heart-breaking and shocking scene of the heinous crime, cruelty ad inhumanity. The half-charred

young girls were playing with the death in order to protect
their modesty. Small children and aged people, helplessly
were awaiting for their death moments. The children of
people were lying in the trucks like the creepers, insects ready
to get crushed under the feet. But, how does it matter? It
was impossible to reach into the ears; the bitter crying of
the helpless children to their helpless moms. Even if it
happens, the moms too were helpless to render any help.
The truck got stopped short of the destination as the road
ahead to be conversed on foot.

But one got the bitter and very painful experience of
that very short journey. Sita jumped out of the truck along
with her one year old son in the same fashion as a female-
monkey (bandariya) embraced its siblings with her breast
jumping from one tree to another tree. Thousands and
thousands of homeless people alike refugees were slowly
marching ahead through the small foot-paths in between
the fields. The people were going through the narrow lanes
the devils (wrong doers) hiding in the fields were taking full
advantage of the situation by succeeding sometimes either
in dragging and killing the children or women getting
victimized of their evil-passion and brutality (haivaniyat)
by way of getting them raped. In narrating the inhuman,
shocking, happenings during that limited period; the writer's
pen (lekhni) very often gets stopped. Ah! the chase and panic
used to get created when the children in hands were being
dragged. Although the chastity of a women was paramount
for the women-folks but the motherly love and affection
for the child quite often would overtake this. After all a
mother shall definitely put an endeavor to safeguard her
own child, who is the part and parcel of her own heart and
soul. Nobody had a courage to turn back and see what has
been left behind. Who had left what? Somewhere, hardly
one or two soldiers (Military personnel) could be traced,
standing with a stick in their hands. There was a continuous
firing either targeting somebody's leg and making him fall
or somebody got that on the head and went into slumber.
While walking, the children would weep often, stop and

wait for their Dads and start running again. The aged women hoping for their lovely sons to return would say with confidence and satisfaction "Now my son is going to come after having secured his daughters". (Hun mera puttar aunda hai bachiyan nu chhad ke). Everybody was running in panic to get escaped from the cruel hands of the enemy. During this period, Sita too was running non-stop with one year old son Bhanu on her shoulder. She was striving to run faster and faster for the survival without giving any heed to the thirsty cries of her son's out of dried throat, "Mom I want to drink water".

The short journey of that narrow lane had cast the shadows of the very long journey ahead. When the people left their homes, they were without any apprehension or worry but, this journey had opened up their eyes that this leaving of their homes and this on foot journey is not going to lay any path of return. Now their ever lived firm belief that the Governments may change but, not the people, was getting faded day by day. On the name of Islam, making the two nations theory as a shield; the fanatics (Staunch Muslims); belonging to the "Muslim League" (Muslim Cadre) had created such an environment that the thousands of innocent people were forced to migrate and say good-bye to their motherland and their country forever.

Till now this philosophy was prevailing that a son can never ditch mother and mother can never ditch son. But, now this fact of truth-untruth was changing to untruth-truth and very often the son would helplessly leave behind his aged mother enroute; with a pretext that Mom you walk slowly and I would be back after leaving everybody at secure place. On the other hand, the helpless mother unable to carry the child, ye, was forced to leave her child on one of the corner of the road under the pretext that your father would now take you along. Ah! With the very heavy heart, with eyes full of tears, the helpless mothers were forced to ditch their own siblings. Oh! the time (destiny) is great and nobody can guess even that what extent it can force the people to do against their will and pleasure.

Another event emerged during this treacherous, awful short journey. An unfortunate women who was in family way and awaiting anxiously for happy movements from the last nine months with the dreams of welcoming the new born, today was taking deep breaths with heavy heart and apprehension lest her husband should go ahead after leaving her behind under such prevailing circumstances. All the time she was recalling the scene of the old woman whose son had left her behind helplessly since the aged ailing mother was unable to walk. The footpath traveller had no courage to turn-back and look behind after having left his / her own siblings which happened to be the part and parcel of their heart and soul. Ah! One mother was carrying her child on her shoulder and the child was crying for water but, the poor mother was totally helpless. After having crossed the narrow lane, there was lot of rainwater got collected in a drain/dump (gaddha) on the wider road. Oh! by taking the big-big steps; gathering the lot of courage; the poor mother drenched the corner of her thin rochet (Duppatta) in order to wet the tender lips of her son but alas! it was too late and the child died out of thirst.

13

The miserable path came to an end. The bridge of Ravi river got sighted which was appearing at that time the bridge of relief capable to get rid-off all the miseries.(Ravi bridge is the bridge on the river named Ravi located at Indo-Pak border). On half of the bridge the Muslim Guards of the Pakistan Territorial Army and on the other half the Hindu-Sikh Guards of Indian Territorial Army were standing. Moment the half of the bridge got crossed, Sita turned around and looked behind with tearful eyes; her beloved Motherland! She saluted the soil wherein, she got her birth and learned to take steps with her small foot. After having sighted Dera Baba Nanak (the last railway station on the Indo-Pak border) she felt so happy and relieved as if, the small child has reached her grandmaternal-home (Nanihal) but, does remember his/ her own house. The people's dark night with full of awesome misery got over and their eyes started looking the day light. In the light of happiness, the people starting seeing their families. Till now nobody knew even his/her own whereabouts & consciousness (Sudh-budh).

Now everybody started searching for their own kith and kins to have an account, who had reached and who was left behind.

Sita too with heavy heart, was waiting for her husband and brother-in-law (husband's younger brother). Till now her mother and brother had not reached. The mind was full of hopes and distress (Shantabhav and ashantabhav).

The four days got passed this way in pursuing the God with prayers and looking for the people crossing the border & Ravi bridge. Everybody after having got free from the worry of saving their life and chastity was now waiting eagerly for their people left behind on the other side of the border. Everyday, with Taimaa (Paternal-grandmom), Sita used to wait for her husband Nath and Mom; at the temple in the morning and later at the bridge for the entire day. The Taimaa (Paternal-grandmom) had only two pillars of motherly affection, one was 'Devar's '(Younger brother of husband) family and the other sole younger brother who was too young in age to her. The life boat of Taimaa (Paternal-grandmom), was being sailed by these two family pillars. She had lost her husband much before the time. Her brother with his family used to live in a small village LADRI, Distt. Sialkot. Moment on the Ravi bridge truck full of refugees was sighted. Sita ran fast and arrived there along with her 'Tai-Maa' (Paternal-Grand.-Mom). The people seated in truck had come from village Ladri.The entire village had become victim of death devils, wherein; the brother of Taimaa (Paternal-grandmom) too got killed along with his three sons. An old man sitting in the same truck, narrated to Sita. Taimaa (Paternal-grandmom)' slain brother's eye witnessed episode as below.

It was dusk, some of the people assured the villagers that a truck is parked at the outskirts of village in order to carry the folks to the safer place across the border. Having believed it everybody accompanied those wrong-doers with cash, ornaments and the money rigged out of the box, hidden underneath the earth's hole. After having advanced further enroute, these wrong-doers (death-devils) separated him and his wife and questioned to their children whether they would like to stay with their mom, or their dad. Oh! what was the fate of the children! A few sometimes were running towards their moms and few towards dads. The three sons of Taimaa's (Paternal-grandmom) brother too opted for their Dad and one remained with his mom. The shocked, stunned women standing like a stone-sculpture were forced to witness the killing of her husband and children. The death-devils; by making the children sit on the chest of their parents; were laughing, enjoying to the top of the glory and mocking by passing the sarcastic remarks; "Lo, look the son-father are making love with each other". The people who could guess the dirty track of these brutal (haivans) enroute, however by hiding themselves could manage to get into these trucks and arrived at this very place inside the Indian territory.

Taimaa (Paternal-grandmom) after having heard this awful shocking episode; fell down like a bird who's wings have been cut; and become unconscious. After a few moments on regaining consciousness; she ran towards Ravi bridge as perhaps she found some undefined pleasure in that very act at that part of time. Somehow Sita and other relatives pacified her.

The people arrived in the truck, told that the police personnel are busy in transporting the people arriving from Pakistan to Amritsar (Indian city). Now everybody had only one inclination (dhun) that let us meet our kith and kins at the earliest after having reached Amritsar. But, it was not so easy to reach Amritsar from Dera Baba Nanak. Due to heavy rains the roads got washed away. Somewhere, by riding the bus and somewhere walking on foot for a while; the people somehow, covered the route to Amritsar. Sita also arrived at Amritsar with two of her sister-in-laws ('Nanads'- Nath's sisters) and son Bhanu with a great hope that her mother and family must have reached there from Multan and Nath along with her brother-in-law (Devar-Nath's younger brother) Krishna too would be waiting for her since long.

Amritsar had become the main meeting destination of displaced and refugees. Sita got totally exhausted by the misfortune of three months' hardships and torture. Children too had become disgusted and parched almost with the life of hunger, thirst and starvation.

The tender child Bhanu with blooming face, rosy cheeks and having been used to drink fruit juice; was crying bitterly, " water, water, water". But, Sita had only one hope and utmost confidence that on meeting with Nath, all the dark and dreary nights full of misery would get over. Ah! Just on reaching Amritsar bus stand, she met with the poor, victimized Bhabhi (Sister-in-law) of Taimaa (Patenal-eldermom); who had lost her bridal coverture (Suhag) by losing her husband and having witnessed the killing of her three sons. Only the youngest son of hers was left for her to live. She was standing like a stone- statue; which could neither weep nor laugh, She bhabhi (Sister-in-law) could not keep the patience longer and broke-drown after having met Sita and Taimaa (Paternal-grandmom) & with infinite agony she cried, "I've been robbed, I've been ruined". Taimaa (Paternal-grandmom) had also been left with these very family of her. Oh! it had now become mandatory for Taimaa (Paternal-grandmom) to remain alive for her grieved, widowed bhabhi (Sister-in-law) and the unfortunate tiny nephew. Ah! thus Sita you got devoid off the company of the most affectionate Taimaa (Paternal-grandmom). Just at the same moment, abruptly, somebody touched Sita's feet. The gentleman was the husband of Sita's sister-in-law (Nath's sister) with whom, just before six months, Sita got her eldest sister-in-law (Nath's sister) married. He started asking, where is our brother, from where are you coming?

Sita could not find any of her near and dear for whom she had come; with a hope to meet them at Amritsar. She with widely opened eyes was looking for somebody all around. Having realized the painful anxiety of her, the brother-in-law (Nanad's husband of Nath's eldest sister) said, "Bhabhi (sister-in-law) I've looked into all those buses, but nobody of ours has turned up yet". Ah! all the happy dreams for reunion of poor Sita; which were being carried by her all through the awful path, got perished into the soil. Ye, all her dreams were shattered. By having undergone for last so many days, the distressful life with full of agony, starvation and torture of ill luck, Sita had totally broken down both by body and soul. Ye, helplessly against her will even, she started following her brother-in-law (Nandoi-Nath's sister husband). As such she (Sita) had to have any kind of refuge. On the earnest request of the Nandoi (Nath's sister husband); Sita's father too along with her family, accompanied them.

As the door got opened, the sister-in-law (Nanad-Nath's Sister) came forward with a lot of happiness and joy. Ah! she got totally shocked and stunned after having observed the painful situation of her bhabhi (Sister-in-law, Nath's wife) and the children, in absence of her brothers (Nath & Krishna). Oh! just a month before, the smiling faces with the blooming flowers of her dear-ones which were seen by her, had now turned into the faded flowers with no glow at all. Ah! helplessly and in disgust, Sita started crying, weeping, cursing (Kosna) and showing distrust towards the Almighty.

Nanad (Nath's sister) along with her family had shifted to Amritsar before the Indo-Pak partition. They had already occupied a house of some of the Muslim family; who had migrated to Pakistan. The house was quite big. In one of the portion of the house, the family of the nanad (Nath's sister) resided and the rest of the portion was lying vacant. Some of the half-burnt doors of the few rooms and the broken window pans of the house were narrating the story of the people who had migrated from there.

In one of the room, Sita got stay-put herself and her family. Hardly, there was any luggage. Just on stepping into the room; abruptly, the thoughts arose into Sita's mind that this room is the graveyard (Samadhi-Sthal) of the tortured soul. She felt as if ,somebody is crying ,weeping and saying, please leave us. We beg for our life and modesty/ chastity (Izzat). The half-burnt faces were being seen all the times & the painful cries, ye were being heard. By putting the break on such thoughts, Sita consoled herself by saying that she would not be staying here for long. It's just a stop-gap arrangement and we've camped here for waiting (Prateeksha) only. She had only one desire while waiting that Nath meets her at Amritsar after having reached safely to Hindustan. Ye now this faith of Sita also started shaking (dolna). Her heart used to get shivered (Sihar) with strange type of fear and probabilities. Both the hopes & disappointments got amalgamated with passage of everyday. Everyday Sita would go to Goddess temple to seek blessings and start wandering in the hospitals wherein ; the wounded, sick, ill-fated and distressed used to be there. Ah! somewhere people were embracing one another happily and paying gratitude to the Almighty and ye on the other side; one could hear the cries of the people weeping bitterly by beating the chests (Chhati Peetkar). Ah! on every morning Sita would get up with a new hope but this hope turned into despair (nirasha) by the end of the day like the dark raining clouds. Oh! everybody's dreams had turned hazy.

Although, the family of Nath's sister (Nanad) was delighted and happy with their good-luck but, the absence of her brothers was a matter of great worry and melancholy. She (Nath's elder sister) was fully comfortable and happy with her husband at her in-laws place. The environment of her house was always full of gay and celebrations. On the other side, Sita had apprehension that Nath had not reached India along with his brother, Krishna.

While standing in routine in search of Nath a trembling voice with full of sighs entered into Sita's ears; "Oh! my daughter, Oh! my Sita" (Hai meri Tiye, Hai meri Sita). Sita saw her affectionate mother with tears, standing in front of her with a three months old grandson on the shoulder. Sita's brother and brother's wife (bhabhi) got left behind as there was no seat in train; but the three month old grandson had reached because he was in the lap of his paternal grandmom (Dadi). The mother with lots of love and affection, embraced Sita and felt very happy and energetic. Each and every part of the body was thrilled and contended with this very reunion. Sita's mother was totally exhausted by body and soul. It was intolerable for her to see the hungry and thirsty child of three months for the last more than three hours. Ah! her son and daughter-in-law (son's wife) were in the clutches of enemy. Ah! at this end, having watched incomplete and miserable life of her daughter, the poor mother got so grieved as if there was no life left in her material body.

To some extent, the waiting (Prateeksha) of Sita was successful as both the grieved sons of mother and daughter got consoled. Also, after a few days; struggling with the destiny, brother and brother's wife (bhabhi) along with other relatives too arrived safely. But, Sita still was waiting (Prateeksha) for Nath and hoping for his arrival there too. Sometimes, she used to get the feeling whether her waiting (Prateeksha) for Nath would be successful or going to remain incomplete. Whosoever and wherever they got place to live, there and there only they got rehabilitated themselves. Sita's both brothers also headed towards Rajasthan. But Sita thought proper to stay-put at Amritsar and wait for Nath. But, how the parents could head to Rajasthan, leaving behind her poor and grieved daughter?

Time was passing by. The disappointment (nirasha) was increasing day by day. The festival of 'Karva-Chauth' (the fast observed by married women for the sake of long life of her husband) came. Sita too observed the fast for the long life of her husband & participated in the rituals and prayers of 'Karva-chauth' by putting vermilion (Sindoor) in the hair-parting, bridal dot on her forehead and red coloured Indian costume (saree). But, after having heard the pessimistic sarcastic remarks of some of the women, she got totally disappointed. Ye, the day of festival of lights (Deepawali)got set and Sita started pondering about the happy festival of last year, which they all had celebrated together and started praying for the similar ones in the future as well. Still, the candle of hope was lighting in her heart.

From the last few days, Sita was observing the neglected attitude and disgusting behaviour of Nath's eldest sister (Nanad). Well, the time was such and it was an irony of fate; that the people had forgotten the feelings of kinships and perhaps left all the norms of relationships, love, etc. while leaving their motherland. Nath's eldest sister (Nanad) was of the view that why they should not enjoy all the comforts blessed to them by their good-luck. Why should they sit nearby distressed, ill-fated, people and bother themselves with their crying of misfortune.

Sita was not feeling comfortable to stay longer in the house of Nath's eldest sister (Nanad). Although, Nath's eldest sister (Nanad) never used to utter a word even but, Sita was able to understand well the neglecting behaviour of hers. But, ye Sita was not in a position to shift from there. Till now she was anxiously waiting for Nath to come. But, as the time was passing; she was losing the inherent strength and getting weak day by day. Along with disgust of the life she too started getting worried about the future responsibilities. With whomsoever, she sits, listen the same dialogue from everybody that now think about future and face strongly the situation, think about the children and what is left in weeping , crying and hence, now face the life boldly. It's not good to cry all the time. God curses too for this very act of crying. It was very easy to utter such sentences by the happy-go-lucky people. Abruptly, Sita got hurt by one more adversary of the nature; as the Goddess in form of a baby-child and icon of Sita-Nath love came into existence in the form of a daughter. Ah! one more adversary got added to the adversaries of the ill-fated people. Moment the poor child came on the earth she had to listen these comments, "What was the necessity? It's very difficult to bring up even existing ones." Ah! what a cycle of destiny! What kind of this irony of fate? What a bad time had come that a mother has to hear these bitter words for her own children. Indeed, such children are unlucky, who take birth during such miseries that neither one gets happy nor unhappy. The innocent child Bhanu, got his younger sister as a sort of toy to play along the whole day. Till now these children (Bhanu & his sister) were playing with the tears of their poor mother but, now they had a new gift to gift their Papa (Father).

14

Ye, the New Year Day! but, Sita had no news of Nath. Sometime, she used to ponder that if he had arrived in Hindustan (India); he would have given an advertisement in the newspaper and if he is yet in Pakistan then how could he stay there till now? As, I do have an anxiety to meet Nath, the same degree of anxiety he too would be having to meet his own "Bhanu" as well as to see me. Like other people have arrived India by getting into trucks, railway trains and joining the column of people (Kafila); he would have also reached the same way. Oh! sometimes she used to ponder lest it's not be so that her Nath should become the victim (Shikar) of death devils; who had murdered all the Hindus riding the train, which was stopped at Kamoki railway station. No, no, it can never happen. I've lost my wisdom by having faced the adversaries and that is why I'm thinking so. God cannot do such a great injustice to me. Ah! sometimes, she would ponder about her those two younger sisters-in-law (Nath's sisters); who had already lost their paternal love at so early age and sometimes about lovely Bhanu who has just learned to pronounce Papa (father). What would happen to these innocent children? But, God can never be so cruel. He has to do justice to the people who have been created by himself. Into these probabilities (Udherbun); for lot many hours of Sita used to spend. Oh! for poor Sita's lone soul ;the problems were numerous and the problems were such that what to talk of having the solution of these odds, even one did not have the strength to think of. The children with faded, dry faces and subdued would keep on seeing the face of their mom, Sita. Though, they always had hope of love out of teary eyes of their beloved mother; but, there was no place left for the feeling of love and affection in the shaken heart, loaded with full of melancholy and adversaries. Sita was finding it difficult to stay longer in Amritsar even for a moment. When there is a strong conviction of the hope; then everything is tolerable and one is not able to differentiate what was bad and what was good. But, when the hope starts getting shattered then the surrounding atmosphere also seems to be fruitless (Neeras). Sometimes, one gets disgusted (Khinn) by having got neglected by the people to whom one considers as one's own and does have from them a few expectations. Having got indulged in the uncertainties of future, as regards her future course that where would she be going along with her four children viz. two sisters-in-law, Bhanu and infant Kiran? No maternal house was left even. All were homeless and burdened with their own problems. Sometimes, she would think to leave the two Nath's sisters (Nanad) with the eldest Sister-in-law (Nath's eldest sister) and let shift herself to her brother's place along with Bhanu & Kiran hoping that by that time perhaps she may get to know the whereabouts of Nath. Next moment, she utters that, no, no, it cannot happen and both these girls (Nath's sisters) shall stay with her only as these two girls were put in my lap with faith and blessings by my beloved Father-in-law (Babuji), just at the moment I had first stepped into the threshold of my in-laws house. How can I leave them helplessly today? What's their fault? Also, Nath would never like this. Wherever and in whatever way I do live, these four children are going to be with me only.

The letters were being received from the eldest brother (Sita's eldest brother) from Bundi (Rajasthan). He too was grieved in the grief of his sister. The younger brother too used to write from Ajmer that Sita should stay with him for sometime. But Sita was not able to decide what she ought to do. Should she stay-put in Amritsar only? Atleast she had a place to stay without anybody's obligations. Until now she had only one aim in the mind to search out Nath any how. As the time was passing by, the ocean of thoughts was getting deeper and deeper. The body had already become very weak, pale, and strength less and now the heart too was losing zeal, will, and strength.

The life ahead of Sita was like a deep sea having a severe storm in it. If, these children are washed away in the storm then where would I search them? No, now nothing is left. She had accepted the defeat from the life and neither had wisdom nor strength to do anything further. Had she had her own house then atleast she could have been sitting there along with her children.

The mother's state was also very piteous and miserable. All the times she used to be grieved with the grief of her daughter (Sita) by having left her own family. Sita would think that she should not weep or cry in front of her and must not lose patience. Many times Sita would vow that she is not going to cry in front of her mother and add to her worries. But, after sometimes the determination of her (Sita) would get perished like a sandunes (Ret-Ke-Gharonde). Throughout the night she used to ponder that now with a lot of courage, hard work and determination, I would bring up these children. But, the determination soon would get baffled (Vichhit) by the storm of adversaries (Vishad) and vagaries of misfortune.

Bhanu was suffering that day by high fever. She was to go to doctor to get medicine for her son. Where and how to go along in an unknown place? Often she would look into the door of Nath's eldest Sister(Nanad) room awaiting her to get up and accompany to doctor's clinic. Even after administering the doctor's medicine continuously two days; Bhanu was not getting any relief in the fever. Sometimes he cried and cried and then became unconscious for a while. Mother & daughter out of grieved heart would curse God for a while and often prayed to Almighty for Bhanu's early recovery. The darkness was all over, the problems and problems were all around, hardly any solution one was able to find. Where to go, what to do? It was like fish fighting for its survival out of water .Though, she (Sita) was marching ahead in the dark night of her life with the light of hope (Jugnu) but she had started realizing that she is unable perhaps even to carry this ray of hope (Jugnu) further.

Ah! the unkind creator of universe; sitting very comfortably, why did you mark all the lines of misfortune and struggle on my palms as a part of my destiny only? Be kind a little bit, what 've I done wrong to you? How long are you making us weep and cry like this? . When the care-taker (Palanhar) and survivor of these children would arrive?

Now, I am totally helpless and only one alternative and only one way is left that I should have a sound comfortable sleep forever by making the end of my life. I cannot tolerate the misery and crying of these children having been alive as myself being unable to do anything. While pondering this way, Sita took firm determination that tomorrow with an excuse of visiting temple in the early morning, she would end her life by jumping into the cold water of any of the water-reservoir. Whole night she held embraced all the children to her breasts in order to put so much love and affection in their heart and soul that they would keep on realizing the same for years to come, though they were going to forget the love and affection of their mother with the interval of time.

Throughout the night, Sita's tears kept on wiping the faces of her two children asleep in her lap. At the time of putting these two children into the bed; she saw her own mother full of love and affection in form of dense tree and bowed her head number of time. Now, this Goddess Mother nature would pour her affection on these children. The happiness would also be showered on these children on Nath's arrival.

Watching up consistently to the children with motherly love, Sita came out for a while and went inside again. Suddenly, heard the voice from her inner soul, "Oh idiot, are you giving this very gift to your own grieved mom- an idol of motherly love? Are you leaving the responsibility of bringing up with tears in eyes, these poor children throughout her life? How the aged mother would bring up these infants? Even if, Nath comes back, will he be able to shower motherly love to these kids? and ye, even in his heart, nothing except the hatred towards you would be left. He would consider you a coward who with the fear of facing the adversaries, preferred to embrace the death."

Ah! having been deprived of fatherly affection, as such these children are looking like faded (murjhey) yellow flowers and if deprived further from motherly love too; then definitely these motherless children will fall on the earth and would get crushed under the feet of the public. Nobody would even have the knowledge about to whom these children belong and ye where will they go? Everybody would neglect them as helpless kids. Without the dense shadow of motherly love and in absence of mother's lap of extreme comforts, these children would never become brave and enthusiastic. No, no I'll live. An infinite and a great courage with will to live, got arose in Sita's heart and under the mother's emotions she picked up these kids again and vowed, "Now I'll live and wait for Nath the whole life". Just a short while ago the same Sita who was thinking to end her life, sat nearby the four kids and started weeping with motherly love and affection. She herself started forgetting and avoiding her cowardice attitude.

She was pondering about the future and was in a dilemma whether she should accompany her parents to Rajasthan to her maternal uncles home. But, there are already so many people who have stay-put (dera) themselves. On the other hand, the family of Nath's Sister (Nanad) has started behaving reluctantly with neglecting attitude as they had left hopes of Nath's coming back safely.

They too started realizing Sita's problematic life and this was quite evident with their attitude and neutral behaviour. To some extent, their thinking and the acts of reluctance were correct as the six months had already passed. Even those trucks which used to come daily with refugees were now coming with an interval of a fortnight and a month. However, Sita took decision that she is going to stay wherever, her parents stay and would keep on waiting for her beloved Nath.

Just then, a thought came in her mind to leave the two younger sisters-in-law (Nanad) with their eldest sister till she is able to make the arrangement of her permanent stay. But, the eldest sister had totally forgotten the sisterly love and affection for her own sisters being indulged in the comforts of her life and she totally avoided by saying that it's not her duty to look-after these two younger sisters and they can only stay with our Sister-in-law Sita. (Bhabhi-Sita).

On the other hand, Sita's mother would pray all the time to the great Almighty for her son-in-law's (Nath) safe return, so that her poor daughter need not to take shelter in anybody else's house. Being a lady of self-respect and witty, she (Sita's mother) too was hesitant to go to her cousins place and stay along with her daughter and four kids. But she was totally helpless.

Just on reaching the bus-stop; some relief came to the broken heart, as the fatherly brother was looking anxiously for her poor grieved sister at the bus-stop. Just on seeing her sister he hugged her so affectionately as if he had found a lost treasure. There was some relief to the grieved, disappointed heart with eyes full of tears; he said, "Oh, my sister for what are you worrying? still half of the people are left in Pakistan and Nath would reach us at the earliest opportunity." On reaching home, each and everybody met Sita with great love and affection; specially the maternal uncles and aunt in whose house Sita was going to stay along with her parents. But, the other people started whispering (kanafusi) to each others ears that, ye, "Ah! What this poor, helpless would do. Where she will go along with the four children? Had Nath been there anywhere, then he could have been back surely by this time." For Sita, such ironically sympathetic remarks were like piercing of the pins into a boil. Sita's faith was great and infallible (adig) and hence, she was not ready to listen such negative and sarcastic remarks.

Sita's heart started recalling the memories of past. The dialogue of the past which she used to take laughingly as jokes, have now started hurting her as the heart-breaking bullets. Once a hermit, having read the Nath's hand, predicted that very long-separation from family was destined in his life. Nath had taken then very lightly the prediction of the saint and on returning home he told the same to Sita and they both kept on laughing together on the old man's prediction. Quite often Nath used to tease Sita on this very prediction and sing , *"Trans Ravi is the home of your hubby, ye trans-Ravi the home of............"* no meeting of mine and yours now going to be," (Ravi paar basera mahi da, Ravi paar basera............ sang hoga nahin ab mera aur tera). On getting a chance ever the naughty younger brother-in-law (Nath's younger brother) would start teasing by singing as; *"Brother is going to England with beating drums............ o dear sister-in-law(Bhabhi), who will take care of yours"* (Saiyan chale England baja kar band o Bhabhi pyari, kaun lega sudh tumhari) All these sayings, trumpets, quite often got recalled by Sita and she would often say, " Oh! God what type of this my life–net karamjaal is; wherein I've been entrapped." In a fraction of second she would rejoice with the hopes and soon got restlessly depressed into the ocean of disappointments. After having reached to her elder brother and parents at Bundi; a beautiful city in the historic land of Rajasthan; she had set a daily routine to visit temple with her mother and children and pray to Gods, Goddess religiously for the fulfilment of her hearty desires.

Sometimes she would go to the nearby park where the people alike her, displaced from Pakistan met and having heard their irritates of misery, she used to get pacified and contented herself that not only she is unfortunate in this society but, there're many more unfortunate, suffering with agony and melancholy. There she used to meet those ill-fated women, who had not only lost every thing of theirs but, also lost their chastity (Izzat). She was totally confident that this unlucky separation of hers & Nath's is short lived for a few days. The words uttered as a prediction by the Saint of "Changa-Manga" were being recalled often that the separation might be of a very long duration, but it's bound to end into re-union (milan). This was the only hope which was making Sita live.

After sometime the situation improved and the peace got prevailed and then Sita penned the story of Nath's missing to her close friend Kalsoom Aapa. Within a few days Sita got a letter from Kalsoom Aapa; wherein she had written:

"Dear Sita, we got shocked at of having known that Bhaskar (Nath Bhaskar) has not met you till date. Mr. Butt (Kalsoom's husband) has put all the efforts to search him but not succeeded. Be patient and do not lose courage. We'll keep on trying to find him out. We have got full faith in our God (Allah) that Nath is definitely going to be found. If found in Pakistan then we ourselves would escort him up to the border of Hindustan (India)."

Yours elder sister,
Kalsoom

Many a time the thoughts would come in Sita's mind whether Nath has already arrived India, if not yet found in Pakistan. If so, why has he not met us yet ? Grieved Sita had become just like a living dead body with no strength left in it, no live breath even. After all, there has to be limit to waiting.

ⓈⓈⓈ

15

In India, Sita's dad and brother had not left any stone unturned and corner unearthed in search of Nath. Now Sita had started realizing that she had lost everything. The garden which was nurtured, had lost his gardener in the world unknown. She used to ponder, "Oh! Sita what kind of destiny of yours? Ah! your destiny during first one & half year of married life had an attainment of unlimited comforts & joys and later not known whose wicked eyes trucked that her boat of life got entrapped into middle of the ocean (majdhar). Hardly, any entrapped boat ever got berthed at the port. When its sailor is going to come ? Oh demit! when the boat is sunk into the ocean then the sailor is capable to get it rescued. But, ye when the sailor himself sinks the boat then who is going to get it at the port?

Sita did not have strength to sail this boat of adversaries. She was searching the candles to cover up the dark path of her life. Instantly, with the passage of electric currents, the bulbs of her hopes got enlightened when the postman delivered the letter, which had been written by her uncle from Allahabad.

Dear Daughter Sita,

Today some ray of hope has come into my disgusted life. Just now I've come to know through my friend that a truck had arrived from Pakistan and there are two young boys in it who are from Ramgali Lahore & resemble Nath & Krishna in age and looks. Beti (Daughter); as I'm very confident that these boys are none other than our Nath and his younger brother Krishna. Very soon I'm going to reach you alongwith both the brothers. Your uncle (chacha)

On receipt of this very letter there was a great joy at home. The children started dancing in joy. Sita too got lost into the happy dreams with full of hope & optimism. The memories of happy – go - lucky life, which they had lived together alongwith dreams of happy future; started awaiting vigorously for the happy and prosperous life. Hardly had this gay time lasted for a week when her uncle arrived with grieved heart, wet eyes & embraced Sita and uttered in choked voice- "My daughter (Beti) please excuse me for having put you in false hopes. All my hopes got shattered when on arriving there, I met those two guys, who had come from Ramgali, Lahore and they were not our Nath & Krishna at all, although, their figure did resemble with Nath and Krishna. Till now Sita had lost only mental balance in her distressed life but, now she lost the tag of bridehood (sadhwa). Sita did have strength to face the cruelty of destiny as well as the capacity to get perished in the mother soil after having got slipped from the cliff but, definitely was not having capacity to loose the pride tag of bridehood (sadhwa), which was awarded to her out of the red shine of vermilion (Sindoor: used for making a spot on the forehead as well as in the hair parting - symbol of an Indian woman's happy state of enjoying covertures (husbands protection). She had this faith that no matter whatever time gets passed; the icon of her bridalhood; her vermilion (Sindoor) is inerasable, immortal and she is ever a married woman (Suhagin) enjoying covertures.

But, how long based on Sita's faith the society would address her as a married woman (Sadhwa). Sita had lost hopes of Nath's meeting in Hindustan & Pakistan. Besides, the will of family; she was bound to follow the customs and traditions of the then society. Oh! merely two years before the same sisters-in-law (Bhabhis) and mates; who under the alter of marriage pavilion (bedi) had adorned each and every part of body of their darling mate with the ornaments, jewellery and beauty aids, alas! today the same mates and sisters-in-law; with trembling hands, were taking out her wedding- bangles. Some were opening her braid and the golden nose-ring put on the nostrils as they didn't want to have any sign of being covertures left on her; which may lead to an objection by the then society. Mom was not able to watch this pathetic scene of her beloved daughter. She had become unconscious having wept bitterly by hitting the head on the wall. Ye, Sita too was looking a living dead body (Zindalash) & was standing by the side of the wall . Ah! the brothers were putting over her the white scarf (A symbol of widowhood in Indian society as 'safed dupatta'). The innocent Bhanu too was crying after having witnessed this pathetic condition of his beloved mother, and saying , "Don't beat my mother. Don't open braid (choti) of my mom". How did he, the poor fellow, know that such a lightening had struck to her mom that its fire is not going to get extinguished throughout the whole life.

How the innocent child, poor kid, who has not even learnt to put eatable into his mouth, will be able to perform the death rituals (pinddaan) of his heavenly abode father? Hence, it was decided that when Bhanu attains the age of five, then this very ritual of post death (pinddaan) would be performed. Sita started cursing herself and started thinking sometimes, that how it is that she too has left hopes of Nath and how her hope got vanished due to intolerable grief of these people. Ye, have you become widow by merely removal of ornaments and opening of the braid by them? In this way, they have done something right by removing those signatures of covertures, as no lady is going to stare (ghur ghur ke dekhna) at me any longer. Demit (murkh-mann) don't believe anybody. You haven't become widow, your Nath will definitely come. But, on the next moment she (Sita) would lose the self-confidence (manobal) and started weeping bitterly all the times after having assumed that her body is a mere skeleton of a cursed-woman. She curses that ill society which had deprived her of all those icons of a covertures, indicative of her bridehood (Sadhvi).

She started considering herself to be lust less (ashaheen) and a burden on the society. She got confused with these distressing thoughts and after having witnessed her deserted (sooni) vermilion hair-parting (Maang) and bangleless wrists; she felt, as if she had lost all the grace and charm of her body.

16

Oh! nothing was left with Sita. Ah! how pathetic it was that she has been left weak by body, gloomy, at so tender age (hardly 19 years of so) with inadequate education and not that very witty even—what will she do and how she is going to bring up these four children? Is she and kids are going to be dependent on others throughout their life? Has Sita, with strong will power, determined to live, forgotten her capabilities to strive under the motherly emotions (mamta)? After having lost her husband; even very bold woman, in every aspect becomes a non-entity. Ye, with teary eyes she leads an accursed life throughout. Pondering thus, Sita curses GOD and sees through her soul (mann ko jhakjhorna). No, no I am a covertures (Sadhwa), my Nath will come, I can't live without him and nobody can snatch him from me. My hopes are immortal. Ye the Almighty is just testing me.

Today, in the evening, the marriage party of Sita's dear friend and cousin sister Raj was to arrive. The childhood friends who never got parted from each other in the past; were going to be departed from each other in the due course of time. Even having been keen to attend her marriage, Sita was not able to do so, as all the time a sound echoed in her ears, "Now you should not attend any auspicious ceremony". If, her attending of Raj's marriage is considered to be non-auspicious, then she should never attend the marriage of her beloved Raj. Raj too could not insist Sita to attend her marriage even though she had earnest desire.

She was aware of the unfortunate status of her friend Sita which had been thrust upon her by this very conservative society. Without Nath Sita's condition was just like a fish which gets enervated without water. As an endeavour to pacify her, quite often Sita would mutter (budbudana) "Now you are no more a tender, sweet, covertures woman in the eye of the society, except a statue of hard-stone, whose life is worthless".

On having watched Bhanu and Kiran playing, Sita's heart got filled with motherly affection (mamta) amalgamated with devotional energy. Ye, neglecting her negative & cowardly thoughts, she affectionately embraced the children by advancing further, as they were the symbols of her Nath's love. So what if, she has lost her covertures but, she is mother still. Only mothers have given births to all the achievers in the world. For nine months, with the energy of her body, blood, flash, she creates the child, nourishes the child with sweet maltose (mother–milk) and why she can't bring up these innocent children with her efforts?

Having relinquished the sweet, tender image of a woman; Sita adorned herself with the virtues like; strong will –power, unparallel capacity of hard-work, unswerving application of mind, firm determination with unparallel strength and true labour as her motto for the remaining life. She determined firmly that the blooming garden which got lost along with its Gardener, would be nurtured by her as the Gardener of the very garden with the manure of the virtues (sanskar) into its root and shall make Bhanu an enlightened personality. She determines to make Nath's Bhanu a shining star (deeptimaan) in the universe and Kiran who was deprived of her fatherly affection; would be omni present like a ray of light. Thus, momentarily she turns into strong willed powerful lady (sabla) and in the next moment again gets back to square one to a depressed lady (abla).Though the dreams of becoming a strong powerful woman (sabalnari) used to get ruined in a moment like sandunes' but, the motherly instinct in her often encourage her all the times to become a powerful woman. While indulged in these thoughts; she received a letter from her brother in Ajmer wherein, he had earnestly requested Sita to reach Ajmer.

Next day along with the four children, Sita with Mom reached to her brother in Ajmer. Brother and sister-in-law ('Bhabhi'-wife of brother) embraced Sita and the children with great love and said, "Beti (Daughter) why are you worried? Everybody is with you and never think even in dream that you're alone". With these pacifying words of her sister-in-law (brother's wife 'Bhabhi'); Sita got lot of contentment (Santwna). Ye now Sita was ready to set-goals for her life at the earliest. Next day only she expressed her views to her brother that she would like to do something in future with his affectionate guidance. The brother got delighted with these thoughts of his sister. He too was not in favour that his lovely sister lives a talentless, distressed life, of a dependent, depressed (abla) woman. Sita's brother found out an organization in Jaipur wherein, only ladies were accommodated and jobs too were awarded there. As a matter of fact, this Institution was opened only for displaced women coming from Pakistan. Sita reached there with her brother. The Institute's officials with lot of affection made Sita aware of the rules and regulations of the Institute and consoled her that by staying there , she would be able to know the whereabouts of her Nath at the earliest. The people who come from Pakistan do make search for their Kith and Kin there in such Institutes only. Sita's mom did not appreciate the living of her daughter in such Institutes. Ah! her daughter was to live under those poor conditions in such Institutions while her brother and parents are alive. But, Sita had determined firmly to lead a life of a self-dependent woman. In order to accomplish her vow; she was ready to stay anywhere in any circumstances. That's why at that moment she got ready immediately to proceed to Jaipur. With heavy heart; in order to fulfil the desire of his sister, the brother too got agreed to this very proposal. He understood the agony of her dear sister.

Now the life of his sister was a long path full of thorns and it was very difficult to cover it up. It was not so easy to face the then orthodox society. By putting the affectionate hand on her sister's head, he said," May God bless that your faith gets true and Nath somehow returns home safely!," Then, Sita asserted to her brother with firm determination, "The sister who is having the dense shadow of brotherly love, like the shadow of a Banyan tree, the power of motherly affection and blessings of father then definitely she would be able to sail successfully the boat of her dark life unto riverbank. Now, Bhanu and Kiran would be here as her pillars of hope to cross over the life—path ahead". With these very thoughts of sister, Sita's brother got contended.

The next day along with mom and children, Sita set course to Jaipur. A few days later; though brother had returned Ajmer on having got all the arrangements done for Sita's stay but, Sita's mom had to stay put with her daughter in anyway. She was not in position even to think of leaving her innocent and the distressed (dukhiya) daughter alone. Just on reaching Jaipur she alongwith her brother visited the Institution. The Director of Institute told that the institute had been established for the women's development. The living accommodation for Sita's Mom as well for her children was provided.

This was the vow of Sita that she has to make the Nath's family-icon (vanshadeep) as the world-icon (vishwadeep). She used to think that this would only be possible if, she herself becomes the guardian as she won't be able to do anything under the patronage of her brothers. Also, she won't let her children get affected by her pangs of separation (virhavedna) and gloomy life . She would wait for Nath with optimistic attitude and not as a dejected or disappointed woman. She had understood well that she can develop the future of self and her children by having stayed in such institutions only. Though the love and affection of relatives, kith and kin's was not there but, the hard work and devotion to duty were only companions in the environment suiting to her conditions. Though Sita had full faith in her brothers that they would never allow her to feel dearth of any kind; but, she never wanted her children to be a burden on anybody and as they grow they get victimized of inferiority complex. After having thus pondered; she accepted the challenge to make the future of self and children by staying in the Institute. After a few days the Institute got shifted from Jaipur to Jallandhar and Sita too took a turn to the new life alongwith others with the firm determination of making the children's future with the hope of Nath's reunion.

In the evening, they reached the heritage (ashram) encrypted as 'Widow-Heritage' in bold letters on the main gate & was visible from the distance. For a while, Sita had the black-out and she became motionless. Ah! thinking that is she widow indeed? Though, the society had labeled her widow but, her inner conscious never accepted this and how it is that today she herself came to this 'Widow-Heritage'.

She ridiculed herself for a moment but, in the next moment a thought came to her mind that if, she does not stay in this heritage then what could be the place where by having stayed she could develop the future of her children in absolute sense. Ah! the God has already got her isolated from the society and now it's good for her to stay here.

In the morning, she had an interview with the Director of the Institute. Having understood everybody's situation and based on their acumen & capacity; the jobs, e.g. sewing, carpet-weaving, spinning the wheel and embroidery were being allocated to an individual in the Institution. She (The Director) said to Sita, " Ye, your age is now to learn and it's my desire that it would be nice if, you complete your studies. My full cooperation would be with you. Having thought this only, I've permitted your mom to stay here; so that when you are in school your mother would take care of your children. Ye, to make your future; your mom is making a great sacrifice, hence you must avail the full benefit of the same."

The idea of studying again appeared funny to Sita as she had left her studies long back and forgotten everything. But, keeping in view everybody's cooperation and the Director's contribution, Sita could not utter a word. In the camp most of the ladies were from Sialkot, Gujranwala, Wazirabad & Lahore region. All were the victims of ill-fate. Ah! some were such alike living-dead-bodies (zindalash) that they were forcibly carrying the burden of their body as they had left behind their alive children crying and weeping (rote-bilakhte) since, they were incapable of carrying them along. Ah! Sita heard everybody's story of agony, melancholy, & witnessed their pathetic conditions with her own eyes and felt that her agony is still very light and started taking the vacuum of her piteous life; a tiny one. While staying in the camp, Sita realized that one must stay among people of his/her equal status. If, a man staying in the hut lives nearby to the man living in a palatial house & multistoried buildings; then he loses his courage, confidence and develops an inferiority complex and feelings of distress.

Sita had now developed confidence that she has come far-off from that very orthodox society where a widow is dejected (tiriskar) and she too is adorned in the white cloth sheet (kafan) for the whole life alongwith the dead body of her husband. Also, her eating, drinking, partying, singing are cremated alongwith her husband's funeral. Sita made up her mind that now she'll stay in the society of the distress of this very camp and make it her battle field to fight the battle of her life (karamshala).

Within a week, with the munificent and sincere efforts of the Chief Executive Officer (Mukhya Sanchalika), Sita got admitted in Surdas High School. The school was outside of the camp. Although, the ladies residing in the camps were not permitted to go out of the camp but, Sita got special permission to book-out daily, which was against the existing rules and regulations of the camp. Mrs. Kaushal, the Camp Commandant was especially happy with Sita's admission and satisfied for having succeeded in her efforts. In the VIII standard, there were tender and beautiful girls with happy and lucky go nature, smiling faces with happy dreams and ye, among them only Sita; too was sitting with a depressed face on the corner seat in the last row of the classroom, Sita was feeling a guilty of herself. The students sitting in the front row were turning back quite often and used to whisper in the ears among themselves after having looked to at Sita. The classteacher had just started enquiring Sita; about her name and from where she had come. Just that moment; the peon entered the classroom with Sita's admit card. The teacher introduced Sita to rest of the students and appealed for sympathetic cooperation. Only Sita knew how, the time got passed from 1 to 4 PM that very first day. Ha! what an irony of the fate that the girl free from studies , Nath's Sita & the mother of two children, was sitting as a student of Surdas School. Enroute to camp from school, if she heard two people talking each other, then she would think as if, those were making mockery of her. The ill-fated people loose their confidence soon and they feel shy even to do good deeds. The same was Sita's condition. She used to think that carrying a school bag is no less than committing a crime.

On returning to camp, the class-scene kept on flashing in front of Sita's eyes, throughout the night. She felt that ye till now she has become the joke namoona of the class only and tomorrow during the prayers assembly of the school; she is obviously going to be target of everybody's eye. Whole night she kept on thinking, would that her Nath meets her enroute school tomorrow and she would start crying after throwing her school-bag in front of him. But, now to weep, even the tears had dried up in Sita's eyes; as if, these tears too have turned their face away from this very distressed woman (dukhiyon). Sita used to feel that going to school was like a drama for her. But, gradually she had adjusted herself to this very new environment. She had won over everybody's heart in that very camp by her nature and good conduct. Bhanu and Kiran had become more lovable toys in everybody's hand.

As such, Sita's mom used to take care of the children, so that Sita may fully concentrate on her studies. So in this fashion, slowly. Ye, the time was going ahead in its own speed.

Now, no longer Sita's mind was wavy (vichlit).Her waverly mind had succeeded in finding out the path of its destination and she was very confident now that on someday she is going to reach her destination. Sita had accepted to suffer with the agony of long separation (virah-vedna) from her own Nath, as the part and parcel of her life. Everyday on return from school to camp enroute; ye, Sita always had one thought amalgamated with a hope of meeting to her beloved Nath. But, she would devote time for her studies and also spare some time to look after her children as well. The lines of distress had disappeared from her gloomy (udas) face. Ah! the God was not yet contended with her compromise. She had prepared herself to tolerate the kicks of misfortunes with bowed head. The Almighty too thought that she has got tolerance to tolerate the kicks of the ill-fate; so why she should not be tested more?

18

The 'Baisakhi' festival in Punjab is celebrated with lot of gay. Sita had forgotten all the festivals after having come back from Pakistan. But, this very year in spite of agony of Nath's separation; sita celebrated 'Baisakhi' with lot of gay and did purchase the toys and garments for her children. After a few days of 'Baisakhi', the senior official from Delhi was to visit the camp. The camp was being decorated in full swing. All were occupied with their assigned job. This was the only opportunity for everybody to display his/her talent. Sita too was busy in stitching a frock (baby girl garment) for her daughter Kiran; as she (Kiran) was to stand with bouquette in her hand, ahead of all the girls who were going to sing the welcome-song. Sita was embroidering the shining glass-pebbles on Kiran's garment (Frock). Sita's daughter was very- very sweet her golden curly hair, reddish apple face with pinkish lips and her delicate hands and legs would attract everybody's heart. Just on coming back from the play ground with her maternal-grandmother (nani); she said to her mom, "mom, mom, Ah! I have been caught by fever". Sita touched her forehead and found that her daughter is suffering from high fever. Having taken her in the lap, with lot of love and affection she uttered, "Baby, its not very high fever, let me stitch a few more glass-pebbles on your garment (Frock) and then I'll take you to doctor aunt." After having stitched the frock (baby-girl's garment); she went to the doctor. She told her not to get worried as this was the mild fever due to the change of weather. So keep on giving her the medicine and she would be all right by tomorrow morning. Whole night the medicine was administered, but, Kiran's temperature kept on rising instead of falling. Although, she (Sita) was tired due to day's work but, still she was sitting very depressed and worried with her Kiran's suffering. The clock struck 12 of midnight and the senior most Doctor of city, a specialist was called in the camp and he too administered the medicine but, before leaving he whispered something in the ears of sister Krishna which made her (Krishna) highly worried and speechless. Very soon the medicine showed its effect and the kid got some relief and everybody went to their respective rooms, but, Sita kept on sitting with Kiran in her lap. Sita too got some relief by having observed her daughter calm and quiet and thought that by morning she is going to be OK. The left over glass-pebbles were also stitched into the baby garment (Frock). At about 5:20 AM, Kiran opened her eyes. As she (Sita)was to put on to Kiran; the newly stitched garment (frock) and hence she earnestly took Kiran into her lap. After having put the garment (frock) on her, she kissed Kiran and said, "Aha! My Kiran is looking truly like a shining light-beam (Kiran)". Happily she called her mom and asked how the frock was looking. Maternal – grandmother said, "OK, now take it out and put on again at 10:00 AM tomorrow.

As Sita opened the garment (Frock), Kiran yawned , stretched her body (ANGRAI) with tears in her big eyes & started staring at Sita. The colour of her eyes and face had turned red. The moment Sita's mom saw the reddish face and eyes of Kiran, she got perturbed and cried, " Kiran! Kiran? Ah! just in the next moment (dekhte hi dekhte); Kiran yawned and stretched her body again (angrai) resulting the falling of her neck to one side (gardan ek taraf loorak gai). Mom and grandmom squirmed, cried spontaneously (Cheekh) and the children too got out of the sleep. Alas! Kiran had slept forever in her mother's lap. Having heard their skirmishes and cries (cheekh-pukar), the other ladies in the camp too arrived there. But, by the time somebody called the doctor, Kiran had bid farewell to all. This tragic incident had shaken everybody's heart. On the other side, there was a panic due to the visit of the Camp-Inspector (nirikshek). Sita was sitting like an expremion (nishpand) stone statue, which had no feeling of pleasure and pain (harsh and vishad). Her mother was cursing the destiny out of madness (akulman). Having embraced Kiran to her blossom, she was quite perturbed and upset (vyakul). Ye, the poor lady having left behind her own husband and family, was here for the comforts of Sita; but, alas! this sad incident made her condition so worst that she did't have the strength even to weep and cry. Moment, Sita regained consciousness & having watched the dead body of Kiran; she started pondering , Ah! if Kiran had survived a little more, she would have adorned her with the newly stitched glass-pearls garment (sitaryan wali fraq) and seen her on the stage with bouquette in her hand, for which she was keenly waiting for the last seven days. Still she (Sita) was not convinced at all that her lovely daughter had gone far away after having left her for ever. Ah! unlucky and helpless mother; sometimes, would try to hear her heart-beats and sometimes hold her nerve (narhi) and start counting the pulse. Ah! the poor mother got so upset that she would start crying in melancholy and mutter in despair, "Ah! Nath has not yet seen even the face of her lovely daughter and how this cruel injustice could happen to us? Sita's melancholy-sleep (tandra) got disrupted only at that moment, when two –three ladies of the camp came nearby her and uttered with grieved heart , "Let us go sister and bury this poor heavenly abode baby (chalo bahno is bachari ko thikane lagao). How long would you keep her holding like this? you're not going to gain anything". Having heard these words, abruptly Sita cried, "No, no I am going to keep this my Divine-light (Divya-Jyoti) for ever with me. Her Dad has yet to see her. Ah! perhaps being pre-occupied with my own worries, I could not bestow my motherly – affection (matrattav) to her and thus with the pretext of dislike (roothna), she has become mute. With lot of persuasion, Sita's strength got revived (dhandas). Instantly

Bhanu came running , embraced his mother and uttered "Mom where are you carrying my doll? Why are you not speaking? Why grandmom (Nani) and other all are crying? If, she (Kiran) is not there then with whom I am going to play and ye what would I tell my Dad on his arrival that where the doll has disappeared?"

After having watched the bitter crying, sobbing (Bilakh-bilakh kar rona) of the poor child; the heart and mind of all the ladies got filled with the deep agony and they too started weeping bitterly (sisak-sisak kar rone lage). The golden haired lovely Kiran, who used to wander in the camp had left forever. Ah! Sita adorned her half bloomed bud (Kali) with the same glass-pearl garment (Frock) as if she was going to bid farewell to her own daughter to the place of her in-laws (Sasural). Along with mom and other 8-10 ladies, Sita having embraced poor Kiran to her bosom; proceeded to cremation ground. Having accompanied from the camp, the old gentle-man Teja, had already arranged wood for the cremation at the cremation ground. Sita having embraced the diminishing lovely doll to her bosom started making the funeral. She was not aware at all about herself (Apni sudh nahi thi). It appeared that she had turned mad due to the unprecedented sad demise of her daughter, since she was decorating the funeral in such a way as someone adorns the palanquin ('Doli) of her daughter. However, to make the funeral was not an easy job for women. One of the old lady said, "Let us seek the help in setting the funeral from those people who are taking bath in the nearby pond (Talab) and had perhaps come there to pick up the remains (Asthiyan) of their somebody .Sita approached them and requested, "Brother! Please make a funeral for my bereaved daughter". One of the persons amused the bathing people & yelled, "Perhaps she is mad. Otherwise how could she have been here to such a place". Sita said with trembling heart, " Brother help me out please. I've come for my daughter's cremation." They had sarcastic smile on their faces. One of them exclaimed, "where is the father of the child? " One out of them passed the ironical remarks, " Friend, had the identity of child's father known then how could have she requested you to make the funeral of her child at this cremation ground?" Keeping the deaf ear to their comments, Sita with grieved heart said, " I have come from the refugee camp. Meanwhile, she heard, "Go ahead Madam, I'll accompany you and also started yelling, " Ye this Pakistan has ruined us all." Having put his blessed hand on Sita's head he affectionately said, "Oh! My sister hats off to you— you are very courageous and nobody felt even slightest pity on you in this very cruel era" (Wah re behan, tu badi himmatvali hai, tere te zamane nu zara bhi taras nai aaya). Sita kept on gazing Kiran lying on funeral. The old man had covered underneath the funeral wood log the icon of Nath's love and the part of Sita's soul- Ha! Kiran with shaky hands Sita ignited the funeral of her beloved daughter and kept on staring with her unblinked (Pathrili) eyes, the funeral fire wherein, all her love was burning. Such an unparallel condolences, pacifism (Dhairya) and courage can be seen only in a rare mother. The lofty branches of the pyre started gaining heights and within a few seconds only, Kiran got vanished from the eyes forever.

19

Kiran's death was a painful event (Halsa) for Sita. Within two hours somebody has crushed the happy blooming bud (Hsati khil khilati kali) of Sita's garden. Now, Sita was not feeling comfortable to stay in the camp. Kiran's incomplete phonetic (Totli awaz) often used to echo into her heart and mind. On receipt of this sad news, the brother too arrived there from home. Having witnessed Sita's sad condition it was decided unanimously that it would be good for Sita to stay for a month at her brother's place. Oh! This hard-hit (Prahar) of destiny made Sita handicapped (Apang) once again. Ye she lost all that self-esteem (Aatmbal) which she had attained in the camp with lot of courage. Now, Sita had lost faith in God. From some corner of her heart she used to listen only one sound (Awaz) that now she has become a widow in real sense and her daughter Kiran too had joined her heavenly abode father. The unprecedented death of Kiran had tremendously shaken (Jahkjhor) her so badly that she got fully defeated (Parast) in the life. The hope of meeting Nath, which was alive in Sita's heart till now, too was diminishing gradually.

Sita had spent a month in Bundi (Rajasthan) at her brother and father's place. But, from the day she cremated her daughter since then the flame was burning in her heart. She started suffering with mild fever. All the time she was receiving letters from the camp enquiring when she was reaching back to the camp? Under such pathetic condition of Sita, no family member was ready to send her back to the camp. Sita too was not willing to go there as she had lost her priceless (Amulya) treasure there. But, she was bound to find out the path for life's destination. Ye, she was bound to live for her two sisters-in-law (Nanads) and her loving Bhanu. Enriched with the great courage to face the adversaries and the society, the most affectionate Camp Commandant Mrs. Krishna, who had picked up Sita, from ground, guided to her life's destination and made her so confident in the very camp itself that she (Sita) had thought to fill up the vacuum of her life. Sita received a letter form Madam Krishna and that letter reverted back all the lost courage in her and Sita got convinced to go back to the same camp again from where only she learned the art of living. Having thought all this she determined that she would go to the camp even alone alongwith her children.

20

Sita's maternal uncle and family of mother's sister (Mausi) had rehabilitated themselves in Mahoba (the land of great warriors Aalah and Udhl) after having left Bundi (Rajasthan). Sita's mom got convinced to accompany her to Jallandhar camp only on one condition that before going there she would be visiting Mahoba to meet her brothers and sister. Mom was fully confident that after having reached there in the company of maternal uncles' (Mama- Mausi) children, (who were of same age group of Sita); Sita is going to relinquish the idea of going back to the camp in Jallandhar. Having smelled mom's desire, Sita alongwith her children accompanied her Mom to Mahoba for a few days. Having reached there Sita's mind again became indecisive (Davandol). The maternal uncle (Mausa) was a lecturer there in a college. A special provision was made by the then Govt. to allow all the displaced women from Pakistan to appear in the high school board examination of that very year. There was no need of producing any kind of pre-certificate to appear in this very examination. So, on the advice of her maternal uncle (Mausaji) and others she too filled up the examination form as she had understood well that only and only by studies, she would be able to progress in her life.

As such in Mahoba, there was no dearth of love and affection in the families of her maternal uncles.(Mom's brother's & sister's family). Sita started getting full cooperation in studies from her age grouped cousins. The

eldest maternal uncle had no issue of his own. but, the eldest
maternal aunt and uncle (Mami & Mama) used to feel their
life full of comforts by watching the children (two sons and
one daughter) of their younger brother (Sita's youngest
maternal uncle). The eldest maternal aunty (Badi Mami)
used to take special care of Sita there. As such she was noble
and broad minded (Daryadil) lady. There was no dearth of
anything. The three sons of uncle (mother's sister's husband
Mausa ji) too were there and the daughter Raj (Childhood
friend of Sita) quite often would visit Mahoba from her in-
laws place in Kanpur.

Sita had special affectionate attachment with the son of
the middle-maternal uncle (Manjhale Mama) who was fully
cooperative in Sita's studies. His complete childhood too
got spent at her mom's place only. His education up to tenth
standard got completed at his aunt's (father's sister) place.
After sometime, on the advice of maternal uncle-aunt, Sita
started residing in a separate house alongwith her mom
and children. Her maternal-uncle had hired one of the house
of two rooms set, on the first floor adjacent to his own
shop. Quite often Sita used to receive letters from Madam
Krishna from Jallandhar. As such she had to visit
Jallandhar once; as whatever strength and courage Sita
had gathered; was a sort of gift of Madam Krishna to Sita.
Based on this very strength, even having lost her daughter
Kiran, Sita had stood again to face boldly the adversaries of
life. Having reached there she apprised Krishnaji about her
future plans that by living in Mahoba she would be able to
achieve her destination soon. Since Sita had left her children
in Mahoba and hence having met everybody and spent few
4-5 days in the camp, she bid farewell to the camp with
teary eyes .As the train started, everybody lost the patience
and Sita too started weeping bitterly (Sisak sisak kar rone
lagi'). She was gazing the soil of the land from where she
gained a lot but had lost something as well.

Everybody was happy on Sita's decision of staying in
Mahoba. Everybody 's endeavour was that there should not

be dearth of anything to Sita and her children. Time to time the encouraging letters with full of motivation (Prerna) were being received from Madam Krishna from Jallandhar. The speed of time kept on increasing with passage of time. After having passed the high school exam. She got appointment as a teacher in the nearby girls school on the monthly salary of INR Forty (less than a U.S. Dollar per month). Thus ,the studies of Bhanu and the two sisters-in-law (Vidya & Tara) got started.

In the evening, maternal-uncles would visit her place, chit-chat with their sister and niece and thus Sita got the feeling of love & prosperity. Bhanu was lucky to get lot of love and affection of three maternal-grand- uncles (Nanas). Having become self-dependent Sita too was contended to think that she was no longer a burden on anybody; but, the memory of her life-partner Nath always would make her upset. Suffering the pain of separation; she always remained hopeful of meeting her darling Nath. Although, she had lost hopes of Nath's returns to home but, some-where the lamps of hopes used to be lighted (Timtimana) in her inner-heart.

Bhanu used to play with his friends & slowly-slowly was learning from them about the unique paternal love which they were lucky to have from their parents. Bhanu too got anxious to have the fatherly love and affection. Sometimes, (Kabhi kabhi), he would put to his mom such n-number of questions as regard to his dad for which Sita had no answers. Sita would pretend to her son by saying that his father had gone to Pakistan to perform his duty and would be back in a few days. Lol after sometime the Government pension for mother and son got awarded and by this Sita got right remedy to pacify her son. On receipt of the pension; every month she would tell Bhanu, look your dad has sent money for you to spend. Thus, the poor child used to get contended.

There was a marriage ceremony of the maternal-uncle's daughter. All the ladies had adorned themselves with colourful garments and jewellry. Bhanu standing in one of the corners and was watching quietly his mother persistently without even blinking the eyes (Tak taki lagaye) and was pondering that how is it that his mother neither had any designer's garment and the jewellry nor she had adorned herself nicely? He approached his mom and said, " Mom, mom, please you too put on the beautiful garments,". Ah! Sita did not have any right answer to his question and at last after having pondered she uttered, " All our luggage is lying in Pakistan and your dad would bring that". Such situations used to be faced by Sita on each and everyday and as a mother she was ready to accept the shortcomings, in her life but, was not ready at any cost to accept any dearth of any kind for her child. In due course Sita was forced to tell the truth to Bhanu as regards his dad. Now, ye mom and son both were in the same boat. Now jointly both started flying the kite of hope and put their heart and soul to the endless waiting (Prateeksha) of their beloved Nath.

Being innocent (Abodh), quite often he put typical questions, e.g. How my dad used to look like? Does my face resemble my dad? Why have you not brought dad's photograph along with you at the time of coming from Pakistan? But, moment when Bhanu understood that my mom, does not have any mark of remembrance of his dad except her mom, then he left asking all this and got ready to face the odd situations along with his mom.

21

With truthfulness, hard work and having considered mother's desire as his righteous (Pragati Path) duty, Bhanu was advancing on his path of progress. Mother too made him comfortable in every aspect; but the thirst for father's love ever remained as a vacuum in his life. Sita got one of her Nath's sister (Nanad) married in Delhi having found a good groom. Sita's life had now become hopeful. She herself had concentrated on achieving her destination. She had learnt to face the challenges. Having observed the courage and efforts of Sita; her mom too decided to be with her, till Nath returned and Bhanu attained the age of 15 or16. The days, months, and years were now passing fast & Sita was continuously succeeding on her path of progress. After having come from Pakistan, Sita had not only lost interest in beauty aids (Shringar Pradarshan) but, also got disinterested in all kinds of materialistic amenities (Bhautik, Aaramdayak Sadhan). She was satisfied with getting her most important daily needs fulfilled. To do job in daytime, weep in the remembrance of Nath during night as well as to study books in order to acquire knowledge ; had become her daily routine. From Mahoba, Sita had come to small village in Bundelkhand region. She got appointed in one of the school there. Truth, duty and hard work were her true friends. The home, family and taking care of Bhanu were the responsibilities of her mom (Bhanu's maternal-grandmother—Nani). When she returned home tired from the school then the blessed motherly love (Mamta), of her mom and Bhanu's affection would make her relaxed and free of all worries. On the other hand ye, she was satisfied with son's education. He was an extra-ordinary brilliant student of his school. Having maintained his keen interest in science, he cleared the post-graduate exam in first division from a college. In whatever field of education he endeavoured, got succeeded. Mom too had the same desire that he must make a special mark in the world of knowledge. She had realized very well that with the education, even the weakest (Nirbal) person can achieve the great heights. She herself completed the degrees of M.A (Hindi); M.A (Pol. Sc.) & B. Ed.

When Bhanu became a major then Sita's mom left for Rajasthan to be with her own husband & family. The youngest sister-in-law (Nanad-Nath's sister) too got married. Sita was now Headmistress of a school & remained posted at one place for the period of 30 years. Ye, in Sita's life ,her truthfulness and blessings of her great Goddess mother were the pillars to her success. She had dedicated herself to the welfare of women-women development. In the students of her school, She too got inculcated, truth, dedication (Nishtha), and discipline and also expected the same from her colleagues as well. She used to spend an hour or two in a week in order to express her views to the teachers of the school as regards the importance of values in life. Sita had understood well, the place of widow in Indian Hindu Society and was well conversant with the piteous situation of a widow. Widow used to be addressed by various titles, e.g. unlucky, un-auspicious non-virtuous (Kulakshani). The right to sit among the married women, to visit somebody's house and enjoy were not awarded to a widow. So far so, even to do Kanya-Daan (Holy oblation of daughter) of her own daughter was considered to be against the religion.

Although the poor widow used to tolerate all this discrimination taking as pinch of salt or even as a gift of God but, at no cost she was ready to accept indiscrimination and injustice to her children-it was beyond her tolerance limit. She rolled out the girl students every year accomplished with full of discipline, truth, honesty, and ethics. Sita's aim was not limited to the class syllabus only. Through so many means she used to be engaged always in inculcating moral values ,ethics, virtues and professionalism

Sita had put the open evidence of women-power in front of the society. With the manure of her ethical values (Sanskar), the water of righteous hard work and duty, She developed the total personality of the students. The people of Sita's domain(Kshetra) used to honour SITA the Christ (Goddess) of the women clans (Narijati).

22

Sita had motivated lot of women to go for higher studies and be self-reliant; specially, who were the victims of the then ill-treatment of their in-laws after having got married at very young age of 10-12 years or so. Right from grinding of wheat in the stone grinder and the massaging the feet of her mother-in-law till late night, used to be the daily routine of these young girls. The husband was not mature enough and used to be enslaved to their childhood habits. Quite often they used to be reluctant to attend the school and were very fond of sweets. After all they were the Prince of the family and ye these young adolescent brides were mere poor daughter-in-laws. If, something goes wrong then along with the other members the husband too would scold and pass the sarcastic remarks on these poor brides. If, these helpless brides were not able to attain the mother-hood after a decade of their marriage then Lo, even for this too, they were held responsible and termed as defaulter. So and so, the parents of bridegroom used to start searching the new bride for their son. These poor brides then used to approach with grieved heart to their parents. If these brides were advised to study and become self-reliant women; then this used to be a mockery as to accept this very idea was almost impossible for them, since they were the married women and had no right even on their own life as per the prevailing customs in the then society. This was the story of each and every adolescent bride at that time. The then society was so man-dominating that the man had never realized that these poor girls had come there on their noble promises. Not only she awarded admissions to such downtrodden young brides, but, she did permit them to sit in the class without having taken the due admission and allowed them to continue their studies. Indeed her real aim was to raise the women's status through education by making them self –reliant.

There are so many examples of self-reliant women-models, produced by her and dedicated to the society as her pupil –daughters. These women are living examples who turned the hatred of the then society into the love and respect of the same society by their hard work and unswerving application of mind. Out of such self-respective, self-reliant and highly educated pupil-daughters, one was Jyoti who not only was the sole daughter of her parents belonging to highly respected Non-Brahmin clan but, later also became a part and parcel of Sita's family just by her dedication, loyalty, sincerity, and perseverance. The young Jyoti who had not even crossed the adolescent age and was still playing the doll-games, was made to share all the household responsibilities as a daughter-in-law in the family of her in-laws. Ye, her childhood got left behind at her maternal place. Just at the moment she stepped into the threshold of her in-laws, she from the young child had become a cultured daughter-in-law of the cultured family. As per the prevailing trend of the then society; Jyoti had acquired the high education by completing her eighth standard in flying colours as an affectionate and a pat student of Sita. Having judged her intelligence, Sita advised her to study further. Her father was very mature, visionary and dead against the orthodox ideas. After having given due thought to Sita's ideas, he while handing over Jyoti's hand to Sita said, "Now onward Jyoti is yours and you mould her as you please." Now most of the time of Jyoti used to spend at Sita's place and she (Jyoti) too started advancing towards her destination. When her husband did come to know that his wife's name has been included in the list of highly educated ladies of the society then he too developed a great respect and love for her and the attention of her in-laws got more oriented towards Jyoti. After sometime Jyoti got the job of a school-teacher at her alma-mater and thus the prestige of the daughter-in-law too got enhanced in the eyes of her-in-laws. Lo! even before the commencement of the vacation; her husband would come from his duty place and the whole family happily together go to their home town.. During this very time interval she had become mom of two children. She kept her studies on; even after being with her family. She had developed with Sita, an unbreakable, pious relation of mother and daughter.

Sita used to feel very lucky and contended in her life by bringing any woman up to the path of progress. Bhanu after having done Doctoral research in Chemical Technology at IIT Kharagpur, had become Senior Officer in the Indian Air Force. Sita got him married in a well-bred and very gentle family. She got blessed with beautiful, ideal daughter-in-law with a pretty graceful face resembling the Goddess Laxmi (Laxmi is Goddess of money as per Hindu mythology), Sita felt as if her daughter Kiran had come back. Whatever expectation she had from Bhanu; as well as all the dreams which she had preserved in her heart and soul, were brought into reality by her able son. For higher education, Bhanu went to USA and also got his mother along. There he toured his mother to the many places of tourism. Sita had already taken pre-mature retirement. But, Sita's this very dream that her Nath is alive and he would be back, ye, could not be accomplished. Her faith did not turn into reality. Thanking God she is fully satisfied today. She truly prays that God may bless her with the eternal sleep within her own prosperous, bloomed family-garden. But, Ah! Even during the eternal sleep, as sigh (Kasak) will ever remain with her unto death; that ye neither Nath died ever, but nor could be found either.

OUR SOME OF THE BEST SELLING TITLES

1. Ignite Your Child's Math Learning

Starting in elementary school, children should be learning beginning concepts in algebra, geometry, measurement, statistics and logic. In addition, they should be learning how to solve problems by applying knowledge of math to new situations. They should be learning to think of themselves as mathematicians — able to reason mathematically and to communicate mathematical ideas by talking and writing.

2. Secrets to Give Your Kids a Great Science Education

Science "happens" all around us every day, and you have endless opportunities to invite your child into the wonders of science. Without expensive chemistry sets, equipment or kits, a child can be introduced easily to the natural world and encouraged to observe what goes on in that world.

3. Who Wants to Teach Their Child, History?

Without historical memory, we miss a great source of enjoyment that comes from piecing together the story of the past — our own, our nation's and the world's. Our historical memory is enriched by our understanding of geography, which lets us better see the physical context of cultures and environments around the world and across time.

4. Recipe for Stress-free Homework

Homework is important because it can improve children's thinking and memory. It can help them to develop positive study skills and habits that will serve them well throughout their lives. It can encourage them to use time well, to learn independently and to take responsibility for their work. But helping children with their homework benefits families as well. It can, for example, be a way for families to learn more about what their children are learning in school and an opportunity for them to communicate both with their children and with teachers and principals.

5. Discover Simple, Super Effective Ways to Make Your Child a Reader

Other than helping your children to grow up healthy and happy, the most important thing that you can do for them is to help them develop their reading skills. It is no exaggeration to say that how well children learn to read affects directly not only how successful they are in school but how well they do throughout their lives. When children learn to read, they have the key that opens the door to all the knowledge of the world. Without this key, many children are left behind.

6. I Want My Child's Success in School

For children to be successful in school, parents and families need to be actively involved in their children's learning. They need to become involved early and stay involved throughout the school year. What the family does is more important to a child's school success than how much money the family makes or how much education the parents have. By showing interest in their children's education, parents and families can spark enthusiasm in them and lead them to a very important understanding.

7. Parents I Need You, Now I am an Adolescent

Early adolescence can be a challenging time for children and parents alike.Parents often feel unprepared and they may view the years from 10 through 14 as a time just "to get through." During the early adolescent years, parents and families can greatly influence the growth and development of their children.

8. Secrets of Astrology Everybody Must Know
(Hindi Edition Also Available)

This book is boon to common man who wants to know how the law of karma affects us. It is the most easily understandable book on Astrology. The objective of this book is to give an interesting insight into some of the fascinating intriguing and mysterious aspects of the oldest science know to mankind. Everything explained with the help of modern science so that it will not look like a purely astrology book at the same time use of technical terms is avoided so that a non-science reader can take full advantage. A fascinating tool to help you navigate through your life's journey, teaching you how to be in the right place at the right time and helping you live in harmony, balance and peace.

9. 'EXPECTATION' (PRATEEKSHA)

The novel 'EXPECTATION' (PRATEEKSHA) is worth to be included in the list of the best novels ever written on the INDO-PAK partition. The heroine of the novel Sita never surrenders to the adversities, never compromises to wrong ethical values but, takes them up as the challenge; faces them boldly and becomes victorious. As a social-novel, its story is very inspiring, interesting, and indulging.

10 ...And A Star is Born

This book has unfolded the motivational and inspirational aspects of cine stars. '.....And a Star is Born' is a collection of the inspirational lives of a few of the Bollywood stars, who kept faith in themselves and achieved the pinnacle of success. All you need is to read these inspiring stories of the stars from Indian film industry. They achieve their goals, although their goals were different from each other. and some may seem easy and some hard. It's a collection of true stories of real-life heroes.

11. Today's Power of Indian Woman

Throughout ages women in India have faced gruesome atrocities. The roles a woman plays in various aspects of life are many. At home, on job, in society, as mothers, wives, sisters, daughters, learners, workers, citizens, and leaders. The world is changing faster than you can imagine and the so-called male-dominated professions are fast disappearing. From Indra Nooyi in the boardroom to Mary Kom in the ring, women have overtaken men in every professional field.

12. Our other Books...

Gullybaba Publishing House Pvt. Ltd. has become a success mantra for distance learners for many years and is proud to serve the students and the needy people looking for quality education. One of the leading publishing house for IGNOU books, having more 400 titles of various topics. These books provide guidance for the exams such as like BCA, B.Ed., MCA, BA, M.Com., B.Com., MBA, B.Sc. Tourism (BTS, CTS, DTS, MTM), BPP, MA, CIC, B.Ed. (Entrance Guide In Hindi Medium, and English Medium), MBA OpenMat Entrance Guide.

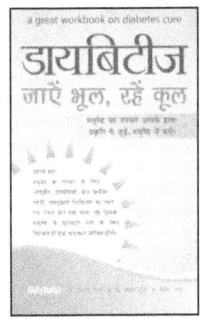

www.ingramcontent.com/pod-product-compliance
Lightning Source LLC
Chambersburg PA
CBHW060833250626
47162CB00005B/2045